THE SITE

"So faith, hope, love remain, these three; but the greatest of these is love."
(1 Cor 13, 13)

[5]

THE SITE

"So faith, hope, love remain, these three; but the greatest of these is love."
(1 Cor 13, 13)

Claudio F. Herrera

[6]

Original Title: El Sitio
First Published by *Lulu* – Content ID684842
First Edition
ISBN Number 978-1-4303-1877-4
Copyright © 2005 by Claudio Herrera
Calgary-Alberta-Canada
CIPO Registration Number 1033647

The Site

First Edition
ISBN: 978-1-4357-3434-0
Translated from the Spanish by Alicia del Azar
Copyright © 2007 by Claudio F. Herrera
Calgary-Alberta-Canada
CIPO Registration Number 1053746
Published by Lulu
Content ID 2776667

http://stores.lulu.com/store.php?fAcctID=81 5337

Prologue

A bad book is as much of a labour to write as a good one; it comes as sincerely from the author's soul.
ALDOUS HUXLEY

For a long time I've looked for different ways in which to convey my outlook on the world, especially in respect to topics related to power, discrimination and religion, and our different stances toward such topics.

As an onlooker I always used my life experience and knowledge, in all fields in which I found myself involved, to analyze behaviour in the face of the different circumstances human actors were called upon to encounter.

It was from this initial viewpoint, of what I call reality, that I put it upon myself to sketch, phrase and paraphrase, my own thoughts and feelings. These thoughts had strong resonance in some of my most beloved persons, and it was they who urged me to convey them to paper.

I must admit that though I never consciously found the opportunity to do this, the images that started to shape this work began, on a particular day, to flow like on a movie screen before me. Also certain changes came about in my everyday life which allowed me the time to get down to writing it.

Although this book does not aspire to great literary value, or the scientific rigor with which an anthropological, psychological or sociological study could fathom the way in which Men carry out their lives and govern their actions, it is aimed to reflect not so much on our doings, as on our frequent lack of commitment to life and liberty.

I, being a part of human kind, live and have lived submerged in a reality moulded by strife of all sorts. Human nature has given us sufficient ingenuity to be able to shun our responsibilities by not assuming them, and by avoiding the realization that the cause of our own suffering has often been brought about by our own silence. This is why it has been very difficult to find the real culprits of the greatest crimes committed against our race; and this was because they were really lying within our own hearts.

We probably ought to have listened to Friedrich Nietzsche more carefully, and not only criticized, rightfully or otherwise, when he said: "It is not force, but perseverance of the highest ideals, which makes men nobler".

This allegory is summoned not only to represent my ideas, but rather, aimed at provoking reflection, awaking individual and collective awareness, so that the day will arrive when we shall be able to say, once and for all: "Enough!", and draw an imaginary line to symbolize that we won't take any further abuse any longer.

The German philosopher Immanuel Kant used to enounce that: "We are all alike before moral duty"; it is this duty which compels us to speak out against any thing that in any way smears our fellow men, for even though we refuse to accept it, our behaviour towards them will always reflect on our own soul.

The character in "The Site" says "You can allow yourself many things in life, but never indifference towards the pain and tragedy of others!"

I sincerely hope you will enjoy reading this book, dedicated to those I love and don't want, as much as I have enjoyed in its writing.

Claudio F. Herrera

INTRODUCTION

We do not learn; and what we call learning is only a process of recollection
PLATO

There was a time when I believed that will was the only motor that enabled us to walk along the path to our place in the world, in case we hadn't found it.

I felt myself as part of something that was in process of creation, like one of the cogs of a giant wheel that made the world turn towards the happiness of humankind. I had the hopeful belief that, due to the joint action of all the members of my community, our future would always be better.

I relinquished my own ideas in favour of those of the group where I belonged, because at that time of my life I was convinced that this was the right thing for me to do. I wrongly thought that with this attitude I contributed to find the shortest way to put an end to, if not all, at least, the grossest inequalities.

I trusted in the intentions and words of my rulers. What is more, many times I justified them even though I didn't fully understand either the reason or the purpose behind their actions. I never doubted that they were in power as a result of my action and election; as I never doubted that their deeds aimed at the common welfare.

It was due to this peculiar way of thinking that I systematically rejected other ideas, other proposals, as I regarded them as alien to "our truth" or "our lifestyle". Who could not want to be or think like us? Most importantly, who could refuse to share our beliefs?

Fortunately, my life is dynamic, not static as I had been persuaded to conceive, and one day all these convictions changed.

When I discovered and studied "The Site", among many other things, I realized that "happiness" does not exist as an individual concept, but that it is a succession, at times discontinuous, of happy moments. Moreover, it also dawned on me that what we call "our history" is the summation of small histories that, despite their apparent lack of importance, have the capacity to make us change our set course a thousand times.

The people in "The Site", its history and the history of my life with them, made me understand that, often, what we call our place in the world is merely a dot. One amongst many others within a universe full of new things to discover, which, in turn, will probably make us change more than once the way we think and the way we regard ourselves, provided we have the capacity and humility to open our hearts and minds to each and all new discoveries.

In "The Site" I learned what a Cyclopean effort it is to our species, self-defined as "Human", to welcome the simplest things that life brings to us; those things which often seem to lack either practical or material value, but which at a certain moment of our lives may become of the utmost importance.

How hard it is for us to realize that not always we find what we search for, and that we have found what we have not searched for at all!

How hard it is for us to realize that the most valuable things in life cannot be found in stores, because they are neither for purchase nor for sale!

We have never had the power to even imagine ourselves walking roads that might lead us to find new truths, or enable us to analyse and reconsider our old truths. I think this is due to the fact that it is easier to hold on to preconceived ideas, based only on our own prejudices and beliefs, or in those of the group where we belong,

How dear it has resulted for us to refuse to admit our wrong doings or the harm we may have caused to others, even though it might have been unintentional!

We live subjected to "absolute truths", supported by allegedly "universally accepted truths", dogmas and rules, and this way of living exposes our uncertainties and fears.

We have never stopped to think that all the bases for our behaviour may have been created by the weaklings to control the stronger. That they may have been the ones that established a system that teaches us how to rest, but never to dream; to suffer the punishment, but never to expect the reward; that is, to not to be.

In "The Site", I understood how, despite being part of a monotheistic culture, its inhabitants transformed a universal, merciful God, into many different gods that refused to grant salvation to the members of other communities because the latter were not faithful to them, without taking into account these peoples' good actions.

This was a society that worshipped dead gods, whose temples had been demolished again and again by their own followers, who often did this in the name of their faith.

We belong to a culture of empty grins, perfectly designed to show our teeth and to conceal our souls. A culture where things are said, but whose individuals are unable to communicate with each other. A culture that teaches us that the meaning of terms such as utopia, wish, illusion, miracle, are unattainable, and phrases like "it can't be done" are drilled into us while other expressions, such as "it can be done, come rain or shine" are totally ignored. In conclusion, we are part of a culture that teaches us "the truth", but never teaches us how to seek it: that teaches us to study, but never teaches us to think.

We live immersed in a system which, on the one hand tells us, and has managed to convince us, that we are free; while on the other hand, it has taught us that freedom also involves danger and that it is convenient to restrain it within limits that are beyond our comprehension.

They never taught us to fly for fear that we might eventually fly higher than them. They could never understand that we can fly without wings and walk without legs.

We should never forget that the world is there for us, and that, by merely using the power of our imagination, we can traverse it wherever and whenever we please, without asking for permission, since it is just for our own will to decide our actions.

Free is the man who thinks himself free and will never allow anyone to interfere with his thoughts. Therefore, I say if they wish, they may enslave my body, but my soul and my mind shall never yield!

The Fall

Death is important only when it makes us reflect on the value of life.

ANDRÉ MALRAUX

Nothing could arrest my fate, or my flight, not even those who steadfastly tried, without succeeding, to seize me, up to the very moment when I started off on my way, with the plain intention of taking my own life, brandishing reasons that to many sounded justifiably false. As if true or false were only linked to the essence of things and not to our beliefs about them!

Maybe unconsciously, and again, maybe not, they were afraid that my fall or degradation would turn into a symbol of their own, by reflecting its image on those who fancied themselves to be powerful and did not dare to look into their own mirrors.

For what strange reason do symbols dazzle tyrants and frighten them with the same or more intensity? Has living in an ultra symbolic society led us to charge expression with meaning beyond our own understanding? Is it because images wordlessly dare to say so much more than what we can express candidly? Is it perhaps that we usually estrange words from their origin, in an effort to justify a non existent rebellion, to prevent to be bound to its consequences?

In a flash, the life which I had thought eternal, and everything, up to the very last thing that supported it, was left behind; and nothingness and vacuum became the space-time which now contained my thoughts, more so than my body, before the astonished silence of my involuntary, circumstantial beholders.

Maybe you have not understood, as they did not, that physical reality, and everything linked to it, had ceased to matter to me in that instant.

No one wanted to hear but they all listened. No one wanted to involve himself with what was happening but they all knew. None thought himself an accomplice, but all felt responsible. No one fired a gun but they all used one. On that day nobody shed a tear, but they all cried.

They all thought themselves supportive, but no one lent a hand. All of them refused to be judged, but they all judged. Everyone valued life but, in one way or another, took part in death. They all spoke of Freedom as a higher ideal, but they all denied it. Everyone believed they were building a better world and together, by act or omission, destroyed it. Everyone, to the very last of them, was victim and executioner, witness and actor.

Many cared only for living... just a few cared to cherish life. Many cared for not thinking, rather than feeling damned by their own thoughts. Many would not be troubled to question themselves, in fear of facing answers. Many wouldn't look into those mirrors in fear of finding themselves reflected there.

How I questioned myself at that moment, when there wasn't time for answers, and I had ceased to be action and turned into thought.

Only your memory and that of others will support me, providing you and they understand the meaning of my act, maybe justifying or just acknowledging it without sharing in it. If not, it will be interpreted and remembered by a few as the logical consequence of the ethical meaning I bestowed to my life, and by many as the desperate and last action of someone who couldn't or wouldn't adapt to the world that was his lot.

Is falling vital to arising? Is fear of facing death crucial to valuing life? Do we have to face our worst demons to value our best traits? Cease to belong, to start to be? Be blind, to understand seeing?

Was my misfortune necessary to question myself during my fall, how it happened that I had not realized before the responsibility each of us has for the beings around us, for our acts and those performed by others, under our express consent or our silence?

Maybe being the offspring of a culture that intended to save itself collectively, exerting the firmest of individualisms, its governing force, I had never before dared to rebel against actions or things that quietly and unobtrusively attempted to control my own life and that of my fellows; even though I knew the consequences they would bring about. How can a drop of water that composes a wave in the ocean excuse itself in its size against the responsibility for the damage it might have caused?

How could I be so blind not to realize that that which was affecting others would sooner or later affect me? That what could destroy them would also destroy everything I loved?

Because of my silence I was involuntarily a co participant of what was being done. In the name of general and individual welfare, I consented to behaviours and procedures that went against my morals and ethics, without becoming aware that it was a question of time before they would apply to me.

How could we consent the interpretation of principles linked to our natural rights, like that of liberty, life and death, in the pursuit of alleged social rights or collective wellbeing, which eventually only served the ones who administered and managed them, even to the cost of our lives and property?

Was it necessary to have involuntarily faced disgrace, to realize that all power is based not on common welfare, alleged to be the reason by those who wield it, but on the drive of a person or group to control another?

How could I not realise the only difference between them was not race, or different religions, or their ideology; but the subtle way in which they carried out their methods to further their own ends?

Let me say it once more; I will never forgive the way in which I cursorily accepted the actions stemming from my pretended leaders and their followers, as a result of not making a commitment in any way, even though I knew these actions affected my basic rights and those of my family! Wasn't their welfare and happiness what I had always professed to defend?

How could I accept to be dragged into conflict, without even questioning what had really caused it, without even making my voice heard, when there was nothing that could justify, but an extreme cause, that Man be the executioner of Man? Why wouldn't I be the voice of those without voice?

Why couldn't I understand that there's a worse kind of criminal than the one who commits a crime, but him who knowingly allows a crime to be committed?

Was it necessary to see others die in order to know what death is and how it can affect us? Didn't I see others live, and be happy, without even reflecting upon it?

Why do we only feel pain can affect our lives, without taking notice that happiness, and its pursuit, can also affect it?

Was my fall, from which I never recovered physically, only spiritually, necessary to realize that being blind doesn't also imply being mute, or passive?

Is dying honourably and valiantly, by any chance, the last resource of those who did not know how to summon that attitude during their lives?

Just like a soft breeze may end in storm or a gentle ripple in a tidal wave, we may understand some day that there is nothing going on in the universe that does not affect us, and that nothing which touches upon our lives will let them carry on unscathed.

Today I can only recollect the good times and reflect on the past; never forgetting your pain will be my pain and your joy the cause of my own. We are many bodies, yet one soul; many roads and just one destination. We are pain and we are hope.

Those from There

"Almost all of our failings are more pardonable than the means we employ to hide them."
FRANÇOIS DE LA ROCHEFOUCALD

Why couldn't they see what was going on? Why had they tried to build a civilization founded upon euphemisms and prejudices? How could they think that they would be able to manipulate reality without bringing about their own destruction, just for the mere fact that they believed in their own superiority? And so on, and so many whys and wherefores that no one could have ever imagined before the coming of the collapse.

I know it won't be easy to tell you in not too many words what happened, but I also know that their lives won't be the same after those events and what they had to live through. Only faith and hope, the ultimate refuges of the soul, will allow them to dream and be thankful for being alive each day, so as to create a new world from the remaining ashes. Whether this world will be better or not, I can't tell, but I assume it will probably be more in accordance with their own nature than the previous one.

They didn't know why they had survived the catastrophe, this small group of men and women of different races, beliefs and religions; hurt and full of mistrust, prejudice and fears. They had become the living memory of the disaster, they were the embodiment of pain and anguish, but they embodied hope as well.

What an irony life is! Many years ago, blind, and after days of roaming like beggars and lost like castaways, the first settlers arrived at this unknown and unnamed place, which they simply called "The Site", because it was impossible for them to feel they could belong there.

Its geography showed, on the east, huge granite and snowy mountains, which concealed the rising of the sun, and endless pine-woods that stretched towards the west, to the long beaches of fine white sand bathed by such quiet, transparent waters that one could see no less than ten huge whales swimming freely in the company of several other sea species. Indeed, "The Site" showed itself as an amazingly perfect place of a breathtaking, almost indescribable, beauty.

All its inhabitants gave the impression of being in a state of happiness and brotherly love, living in their different localities in harmony with other species, many of which, like them, once had been on the verge of extinction.

The people of "The Site", referred to themselves as "Those from There", while stretching their arm and pointing to all directions, probably in an unequivocal way to deny their reality and to feel apart from each other in the endurance of their misfortune.

Their disgrace didn't prevent them from meeting every sunset, with their families and other friendly families; all of them in silence, their faces turned towards the sun. Maybe this was an attempt to feel through its warmth, the presence of that sunlight they could not see, a fact they had not quite come to terms with, although they had had to accept it, just like everything that had happened to them.

"Those from There" were governed by a ruling class, which they called "We", and had appeared in the earlier days, resulting from democratic elections held in the different localities, whose inhabitants had voted for their representatives.

These people lived in different communities, located in perfectly bounded areas, surrounded by plants with colourful flowers and imposing woods. The communities had different names. The one in the north was called "The Blacks"; in the mid-east, among the mountain woods, lived "The Whites"; "The Yellows" were in the mid-west, by the sea and "The Others" in the south. These settlements were interconnected by multiple roads and paths, where one could always see people travelling back and forth.

At first, I assumed that the names of the communities were just some kind of classification; otherwise, I couldn't guess what they meant. However, I couldn't help being puzzled by these denominations, and by the scornful manner used by the members of each community when referring to the inhabitants of the others, which I felt proved that the publicly expressed friendliness between them was mere pretence. .

All the buildings in the different communities were practically identical small rectangular houses with mud walls and wooden roofs; their doors and windows looking westwards. The houses in "The Others", however, were round in shape. All these people's customs and foods were alike, as well as their clothes and footwear, which they made with fibres and furs from the region. There was similarity everywhere, with the exception of the underlying scorn they felt towards the members of the different communities, which was identical and widespread.

The "We" lived together, regardless where they had come from, in an oblong building surrounded by a tall wooden fence, called "The Centre". Its most striking features were the smallness of the doorway and the fact that all the windows opened to an inner court.

All these places, without exception, were inhabited by people belonging to different ethnic origins, either pure or showing a mix of races.

"Those from There" had almost identical build and character. They were of medium height, strong and surly. "The Others", however, were much taller and slimmer, sinewy and sociable.

All of them were blind, but during my stay there, I noticed that the few members of the ruling elite could see, albeit their eyesight only allowed them to recognize shadows, and this minimal advantage was enough to enable them to exercise control over the rest.

The elite from "The Centre" made all the decisions regarding the government system, security, education and justice. Together with the religious authority of each place, also belonging to the ruling class, they established the necessary parameters to avoid conflict between the different communities and to see to the "common welfare", which was nothing but what they themselves considered as such.

The families were apparently organised in a patriarchal structure, but it was actually the women who were in control. In most cases, they consisted of a couple with two children, living under the same roof.

The children of the community enjoyed a privileged position. Their parents had to ensure their well-being and the "We" were in charge of giving them a suitable education. In the absence of parents, the ruling elite assigned these children to foster families that had been carefully chosen to look after them.

The inexistence of elderly people was a remarkable feature in this society. However, with the passing of time, I learned that, without exception, their sons and daughters sent them to a place especially designed for them where, I was explained, they would get everything they needed . . ."with the exception of love", I thought. Of course, the reason for creating this place was to rid themselves from the troubles and cares required by the old.

The younger generation had found a socially accepted way to stay apart from the degradation and death of their parents, leaving aside all recollections of their childhood and gratitude for the devotion and dedication that they had bestowed upon them in the process of their growth into adulthood.

At first, I couldn't understand what I regarded as an evil scheme. I couldn't understand when or in which circumstances, they proceeded in this manner, detaching themselves abruptly from their parents, with the consent and justification of the "We", since they had been the "centre of the universe" for their progenitors

Each time I enquired about the reasons for this behaviour, I received so many that I honestly couldn't take them in, much less analyse them. Therefore, I concluded that when one resorts to countless reasons and excuses to explain certain behaviour, it is almost certain that one has none.

Why do we always seem so ready to rant about that which we lack? There are always so many reasons to talk ourselves out of assuming our responsibilities!

Another distinctive trait of these people was their unlimited greed to collect different objects. For example, those from "The Blacks" loved round stones, while "The Whites" coveted square ones, "The Yellows" preferred sea snails, and those from "The Others" made 10cm x 20cm pieces of wood. Was this an attempt to prove their self asserted superiority over the other communities?

"Those from There" devoted most of the day, together with the other members of their respective groups, to the collection, building, counting and storing of these precious objects, which they put inside wooden boxes, especially made for this purpose and which they kept in their homes under strict custody.

This hoarding of stones, snails and boards was probably the means by which they showed their power, either within their community or to the other communities, for in "The Site" nothing could be bought or sold.

Even though "The Others" were agnostics," Those from There" professed a deep religious belief; albeit their religions differed, depending on the community to which they belonged. For example, "The Blacks" defined themselves as Jews; "The Whites" said they were Catholics, and "The Yellows", Muslims.

Given the fact that each community regarded its religion as the real one and, without exception, all their respective inhabitants stated: "Our God has preserved us from our impending doom". Moreover, they refused to admit that there was some truth in the teachings of the other religions. They hadn't realized that the roads to God cannot be shown in any map!

There was no questioning regarding the infallibility of the religious authorities and each and every community had relinquished to them absolute monopoly to communicate with the God that they worshipped as the only and true one. These authorities determined what was morally right or wrong for their congregations. They also imposed the rites and they saw that these were observed strictly in the places designated by them to this effect, which had usually been built in the centre of each locality.

The religious authorities had managed to make people believe as a dogma that it was more important to belong to, and practise their religion in all its forms, than to walk the path towards whichever God they believed in, by means of their good actions. Of course, these theological authorities had in this manner subtly consolidated their power over the other members of their communities.

During my stay there, I understood that "The Site" neither had nor needed external enemies, because these dwelt within the hearts of its members and organisations. As regards these feelings, we may sometimes assume that hate can often be useful to achieve certain purposes, but we should always bear in mind that it will never serve us to build anything that will survive us with dignity.

My Tiny World

It is unfair that a generation be compromised by that preceding it. We must find a way to preserve coming generations from the avarice and inability of the present ones.

NAPOLEON BONAPARTE

How many times have I wondered who wouldn't have wanted to live in "The Site", when knowing its entire surface was of a balance and beauty impossible to describe.

Maybe the surroundings where I grew up, in this so called "perfect" society, didn't allow me to understand that, like a gyroscope, only certain conditions alien to it enabled the preservation of its balance, taking into account that its nature was defined by its own imbalance. We evidently lived within an incredibly unstable equilibrium.

It is impossible to forget the happiness we both enjoyed while walking barefoot along the beaches, arm in arm with her, enjoying the water wetting our feet, the sound of the sea, the children's laughter; the simple but profound things like her smile, the softness of her skin, the relaxed sound of her voice, or the sun gentle touch of the sun; all this that had achieved what nothing else had; it had made me think it could be quite similar to the warmth I must have felt in my mother's womb.

How could I not recollect our hikes through the woods or the mountains, only now and then stopped by our small talk?

How could I not remember the gentle breezes that flooded our senses with the diverse aromas that filled the place?

If we so chose, it was only up to us; we could listen even to the sound of silence, or the wind whistling through the leaves and the trees, or the noises made by the people of the place, no matter how little; or the singing of the brooklets running downhill, yearning for the ocean, hardly waiting to reach it; or the sound of our footsteps, sometimes slow... other times not so slow.

How could I forget my frequent trips to different spots within "The Site", always under the silent scrutiny of many of its inhabitants and the suspicion of its authorities?

How could I forget that the only purpose of my stay in other communities was to visit a good number of friends and acquaintances I had made during the passing of days, little by little and without realizing? The bond that linked us was way beyond many reasons, which some invoked and we ignored; reasons wielded in order to avoid any sort of contact that could strengthen any relationship between the inhabitants of the different places.

How often have I spent the night in their homes, and they in mine? How many times did night take us by surprise, sharing our food, our lives, our dreams, our happiness, our laughter? How often did the first light of day find us conversing animatedly on this and that, not minding anything else? How many times did we cease to be individuals and became us?

[38]

How many times in an effort to help someone in his task within his community, did we collaborate generously side by side, as equals, gathering objects valued by the group, or helped in their making, enjoying those fraternal moments?

We never stopped regarding and respecting ourselves as equals, without minding any criticism, often hurtful and offensive, from those who thought differently. We had understood that like the bricks, whose fortitude lies in a structure, our greatness lay on what we could achieve side by side. Who thinks of a brick while seeing a building? But, what would become of that building, without bricks?

We had expressly agreed, to avoid any unnecessary tension between us, never to speak critically, much less, demeaningly, about subjects linked to the government of the different places, or their religious beliefs, or habits, their dominating doctrines or their flaws, though we thought these had an effect on the lives of their inhabitants and could be solved; unless those who could be affected by such commentary agreed or had openly enquired on these subjects.

Even though there was a multitude of things we did not understand regarding the behaviour of our leaders, and the shady way in which certain affairs were managed all around us; even though complaints were raised, and rapidly silenced, we firmly believed the way of life established by "We" in "The Site" was little short of perfect. We weren't blind as a result of circumstances, we were blind by conviction.

If there was one thing my friends from "The Blacks", as well as "The Whites" or "The Yellows" or "The Others", agreed upon fully and without a doubt, was that the way of life dominant in "The Site" generally, and in particular, evidenced in their inhabitants' practices, had been able to overthrow the trap set by the mechanism of the long gone preceding generations... the control and measurement of time as a system to run their lives.

Many regarded counting the hours as not only normal, but part of a process aiming at the attainment of a more organized community, whose performance would result in the increase of material wellbeing for its members; as though this were the most important thing to Man as a social and spiritual being. No one realized how, little by little, this system turned into a trap destined to do away with their freedom and restrain their creativity.

Everyone without exception was entered into a goods production system, where Machine, in different guises, periods or names, became the very heart of the organisation, and the people one of its vital parts. They were never considered less than machines... nor did they ever become regarded above them.

It was not Machine, which could not stop functioning when it chose to, or follow the dictates of our inner, natural clock, the one which adapted itself to the flexible system that had previously ruled the lives of men, stemming from their own nature; it was they who had to strictly follow its pace.

It was during these times when such terms as "creative idleness" were left behind, among others, because the new system rendered them unimportant and also enemies of a so called efficiency. Idleness in any form was unacceptable and its only mention was condemned by society. You had to be "productive".

This mechanistic concept, like other ideologies stemming from it, had sprung from the quest of a system beneficial to many through the effort of a few; however, at length, it eventually favoured a few through the effort of many.

The new philosophy had not only achieved that man became a necessary part of Machine for the manufacture of different goods, but had also made him receive, for being part of the industrial process, another product, originated from other machines and the work of other men in like manner; which was called money.

Money, which had been assigned an ideal, conventional value, was basically set aside for the purchase of goods that other machines and other men produced. This was a machinery that in a certain way fed back on itself.

There came a time when the system started to abstain from employing people in favour of more recent technological developments, and began to cast them away; they and the outdated gear they had served, without guaranteeing the means to come by the products that the system itself, in a previous stage of development, had assured were essential to their lives or, to improve their "quality of life".

Many had to change their time systems once more, in order to survive within the new technological order, readapting their biological clocks, to further processes referred to as flexible.

The mechanics of hours had silently grown, like many things do, to dominate their lives. There was a time to produce, a time to rest, a time to go back to produce, a time to go back to rest. . .

Everything, in this era of artificially illuminated spiritual darkness, was conceived in terms of "increased productive performance" and the attainment of happiness through the obtainment of certain material goods, and very little in function of obtaining a significant betterment in the quality of life of those participating in the system.

Everyone could set their lives to the ticking and whirring of different equipment, created to prevent workers' late arrivals and delay in taking their stations within the process. This equipment, in one way or another, served to alter internal clocks, adapting them to a new cycle of pre-accorded time.

The influence of the system was so great that practically all members of this society came to think that it was really part of their own nature.

The concept of time, and its control, became so important that everything was valued and measured according to it, to the point that people started to believe that the passage of time made them older and, like machines, less productive or less efficient than other members of society or new elements and processes, drawing them nearer to their time to die.

The current system prevented them from realizing that, regardless the passing of seconds, minutes, hours, days, weeks, months or years, growing old and even dying, started the very instant in which one began counting time, or losing dreams or illusions, or the aptitude to feel part of the future, that instant of time where anything is possible. No one understood that this was what made it possible to see very old people, though seeming young, and also very young people, though seeming old.

No one understood that to be born and to die are mere accidents, such as the past, the present and the future.

In Search of Answers

Know thyself.

Accept thyself.

Excel thyself.

St AUGUSTINE

At first, it was quite hazardous to establish communication with "Those from There". This was not only due to the evident control that the "We" had over all the people in their communities, but also because it was impossible to bridge the gap established by their fears and my impossibility to understand their open displeasure when I answered the questions with which they invariably started their conversations, "What's the colour of your skin?", "What's your religion?"

I just couldn't understand why, especially when I tried to approach the inhabitants of "The Blacks", "The Yellows" or "The Others", and any of them enquired about the colour of my skin, the fact that I said it was white should cause him to insult me and walk away, making angry gestures.

This embarrassing situation changed one day when, with the excuse of finding out about something he had lost, a man from "The Whites" came to me. His name was Pero, his colour black and his countenance serene.

After this initial approach, he started making the usual questions regarding my colouring and religion. Therefore, after my previous experiences, I answered rather meekly, "white" and "Catholic", but contrary to what I had supposed, Pero smiled, as if his expectations had been completely fulfilled; he took my arm and in a friendly way asked me if I liked the place and, to my amazement, whether I wanted to know his community and its members. While we walked slowly, arm in arm, Pero showed great interest in my presence there and kept asking me questions such as "Where are you from?" "When did you arrive?" "Is there anything beyond "The Site?" and so on, but I tried to avoid giving him any answers.

I was so aware of how morose "The Whites" were that I was really surprised by Pero's smile, his suavity, his whispering voice and, most of all, his deeply felt religion.

The friendliness with which he treated me resulted in my moving to his home. During the first days of my stay there, we spoke about general topics regarding the place and its customs, in a way that served us both to gain each other's trust.

Eventually, Pero, maybe unintentionally, turned out to be the bond I had been searching to get closer to any of the groups and to find explanations and reasons for many things I had noticed there. My main curiosity was to find out why the members of the communities of "Those from There" had arrived at that backward situation, since it seemed to me that they were cultivated and wise people. Had it been their choice, or was it the result of some ghastly experience they had suffered? Where did they come from?

After having lived there enough time to get to know them quite well and when, on their part, they had left aside their initial fears and felt comfortable in my presence, I decided to show my interest in learning more about them openly and my need to find out the reason why they were there.

The second time I made some straightforward questions about these issues, I perceived a weird atmosphere because, even though it was evident that they all were willing to speak, no one dared to be the first to come out with an answer. It was evident that I had opened a door they were all afraid to cross. We can be so scared to do what we are not forbidden to do!

Pero was the first one to speak, I think he felt the anxiety and restraint that prevented the others from saying what they were willing and wanting to communicate, and he had realized that the moment had come to help me, and at the same time, to encourage the others to express themselves. However, he was not quite at ease either, since when he began to tell the history of his forefathers, I noticed that he spoke slowly and warily watching my reactions to his tale.

He said that as far as he knew, and had been told, his origin, as well as that of all the other people in "The Site", was a civilization from the other side of the mountains which, in spite of its technological development, had been obliterated by a virus, probably the same that had blinded the few survivors who had become the first inhabitants of "The Site".

It is worthwhile mentioning that I heard this same story, repeated almost automatically by the inhabitants of the other communities, whenever I managed to make contact with any of them.

While I was listening to Pero's story, I noticed both in him as well as in the other members of his group that feeling of nostalgia and longing for a lost perfection that we all experience for the things we no longer have.

"Those from There" were never able to understand or try to find out the reasons why that much missed and idealized society, where everything had been ruled and regulated towards the general welfare, had caused its own destruction.

How could I explain to them, make them understand that more than often, societies, like individuals, have the capacity to commit suicide, just because they are constituted by human beings?

Time passed, and as I listened to their daily stories, they lifted the barriers that had initially kept us apart. Then, one evening, while Pero was speaking, one of the men, of clearly defined oriental features, slowly drew towards me and very discreetly gave me a big basket covered with a tight lid.

My first reaction was to thank him in a whisper, to ensure him of my discretion, even though I had no idea that its content would become of utmost importance to assist me in my quest, so I waited to open it when I was alone.

There are no words to describe my wonder when I found that the basket was full of yellowish magazine and newspaper cuttings, as well as different kinds of writings, manuscripts and photographs of the old civilization.

It took me some time to get over my elation at having come across such valuable material, which had probably been hurriedly collected at random, preserved and brought to "The Site" by those blind people that couldn't see what they had saved in their flight from the disaster.

Those distant survivors, running away from adversity, had realized that their blind and sad wandering had brought them to a place of no return. They would never again be able to go back to those places that had seen them being born, brought up and, eventually, leave forever. Everything they had known and lived had now become nothing but a memory.

With the verbal information I had compiled during those weeks, and after carefully classifying the written material I found in the basket, I devoted myself to find out the reasons for the catastrophe and the, from my point of view, outrageous differentiation that these people made between them and the other communities and their inhabitants. I also wanted to learn why they were so religious and why they had different creeds. Furthermore, I wanted to know why they had chosen this place, where they had come from and, above all, where they were going to.

My Small World

Our desires in life form a chain,
whose links are hopes.
LUCIUS ANNEO SENECA

How many questions you had to make and how many answers I had to silence, knowing I should not disclose that which inevitably, sooner or later, you would have to discover on your own.

How could I explain how difficult it was to "Those from There" to live within a society of blind men, and to understand and accept many things in their lives which happened and they could not see?

I had so many questions to make to you too, and you, sometimes with your best manners and other times using your excellent sense of humour, knew how to courteously avoid answering, not even granting the space or chance to repeat or rephrase them.

It has always been impossible for me to forget our first meeting, and how funny your voice seemed to me, halting and soft with amazement, unable to utter clearly those first words. Maybe your fears and emotions prevented you from doing so. Maybe you never imagined that our encounter, which was not fortuitous, could have been possible.

Do you remember our first strolls through the place of "The Whites", and also our trips to other parts that made up "The Site"? During which, notwithstanding my profound silences and evasive looks, you never gave up asking me, among other things, why I was there, where we had come from, how, why and when. Do you remember?

I remember your simple clothes, your supple, quick gait, as if time were running against you and, especially, the sparkle in your eyes and almost imperceptible smile, in response to each evasive answer I gave you.

How could I forget "The Whites" homestead, and the small valley where it lay, surrounded by grey mountains which rendered the feeling of being endless and eternal... as if they had always been there. Mountains covered in a dark green shroud, from the vegetation that partly draped them?

How to forget the great woods of age-old pine trees, surrounding everything, their deep color, their peculiar scent and that special feeling of heat, cold and dampness I felt as I walked among them?

Few know that many times as I walked far into the paths running through them, I experienced the rare feeling of no longer fearing the ability to enjoy my faculties and emotions to the full.

How could I forget that strange pride, shared by all those inhabitants in "The Whites", of being the closest place in "The Site" to where the first settlers arrived to create it?

We had become, with the passage of time and by decision of "We", the keepers of the only road that led to the other side of the mountains. This road was forbidden to all those that ventured to pass through it, making trespassers liable to be punished by the authorities in exemplary manner.

Do you recollect the long rows of people, of different ages, sitting in wait for the sun to set, and how at a certain hour the streets near the place of worship became impassable, because of the number of dwellers marching towards the same spot under the observant control of "We"?

How could I forget the sweet smell of food which ensued from their homes, at a certain time of day, filling every corner of the community? How could I forget *Matuca*, and that feeling of wellbeing and content when eating it; sitting on the floor of our homes on vegetable fibre mats and tasting that dark, sweetish, thick stew made from mushrooms collected in the woods, flowers and sundry game meat?

How could I forget the cosiness of their homes, and particularly my own, with its great windows facing the sunset; its kitchen, which we had turned into probably its most important part, its furniture made of thick wood and, especially, that feeling of security we experienced from being together, protected by the thick, terra cotta coloured walls, and by our smiles.

How could I forget the voices of my children, and that personal relationship we had, which went beyond incidental disagreements; our meaningful looks or dialogues, which frequently proceeded in silence? I could never grasp which was the decisive moment when we as parents, unknowingly and without warning, turned from being considered a binding point of reference to our children's comments, judgments and praise... to become the exact opposite.

How could I forget the fragrance of their hair, the softness of their skin, the colour and sparkle of their eyes and the melody of their voices, since we were able to corroborate our love, without words, only by running our hands over our faces?

Do you remember that day when you and I were leaving on a trip through the place of "The Yellows" on the coast, when she, as she walked hugging me to the door of our house, with her head on my shoulder, after kissing me softly, whispered my name in my ear, but with that firmness which can only be conveyed by that who is extremely in earnest, and pressing her body to mine said, "Do you know why I'm not grieved and don't try to prevent your leaving? Because I know that love is like fire and though we mustn't forget to feed fire we mustn't deprive it of oxygen... and we are fire!"

Do you remember how her eyes and mine filled with tears as she said this and I heard it?

Did I ever tell you I felt she could kiss me with just a glance, and that to me the word love would have been impossible to define without uttering her name?

As regards "The Yellows", I will never forget how their city on the blue waters of the bay impressed you, with its sizeable buttresses and its great doors; its wide well trafficked streets; its people in colourful clothes, but similar to other communities, their snapping, guttural speech, their utmost discipline, their white houses, wide market places and great fish stores, where the produce of the inhabitant's joint effort, and that of their small boats, was proffered.

You could never understand the reason why they never trusted you, even when you tried to no avail and more than once, to speak to them as equals, in the style of someone who felt great respect towards their customs and traditions. Maybe you never stopped to think that the way in which you analyzed things, prevented you from understanding that, more important than what they could have said to you, was to become aware of their reserved way of thinking. They communicated through their silence, through their "not saying".

It has always been funny to recollect your grimace of disgust when you first tasted Bakuni, in an effort to win their friendship, and how you enthusiastically told them you loved it. You didn't know that they alone ventured to prepare that rare, evil smelling fish.

How could I forget how your hearty laugh resounded in the place we were visiting; creating surprise and bewilderment in those present, when I whispered to you, indicating them, and what they were eating, that you couldn't trust people who ate such filth with pleasure.

During that trip it happened, in that crossroads, next to the stream where we had stopped to rest in the balmy shade of some low trees, that you met that woman who impressed you, and caused our parting because of your desire to accompany her to her town in the south.

I remember how neither my warnings about the difficulties you could encounter on the road, or the dangers you would have to be prepared to face. Indeed, there was a tense situation between her community and the rest breeding at the time, which, though still slight was likely to take a turn for the worse.

Heart, as it is often wont to do, had turned you away from the road reason would probably have set as correct.

I can't describe the deep pain it caused me, after several days' absence, to see you arrive so silent and sad, as if something in your life had stopped at a point where there was no turning back, although it could have been possible. Perhaps it was during your stay in "The Others", next to the woman that had conquered your heart, when you understood that the kiss which is most difficult to give, and the one that awakes more emotions in us, is not the first, but the last.

Seeing you were so crestfallen, and knowing you to be so energetic and passionate in everything you engaged in, decided me to take the personal risk, which to an extent also involved my family and loved ones, of planning and organizing meetings for you, more often than usual, with my friends and members of my community, under the protection of our silence, and of my house and family.

The one thing that mattered to us in those days was that, through the renewal of your search you would forget that love that continued to speak inside you, despite the distance, and your knowledge that the occasion to enjoy it was only the product of your desire, not of reality or your will. Your love, but not hers, dwelt further than distance itself.

It would be impossible to describe the happiness we felt when we knew you were impressed by the objects we silently and discreetly gave you, on that night, avoiding to come out in the clear and to make it apparent to you, how we performed this act, that we really sensed it was very important to you... and to ourselves.

Your thrill and happiness were indescribable, and were, though you probably didn't realize, also our own.

They never had the chance, neither did I, to tell you it was your questions and words, even the ones we did not answer, what made us ask ourselves many other questions, to which we were not able to find answers. It was the trust and the liking we gradually started to feel towards you, what made us decide to do what we did on that opportunity.

We had all silently agreed and accorded that it was preferable, the worse coming to the worst, to regret having done what we wanted, than later regretting what we, wanting and desiring to do, hadn't done.

The Origins

Wise men ne'er sit and wail their woes, But presently prevent the ways to wail.

WILLIAM SHAKESPEARE

The first settlers in "The Site" were part of a civilization that had dwelt on the vast plains across the mountains. This society regarded itself as modern and progressive, and a strong feeling of admiration and gratitude for its scientific and technological development ran deep in its people. They believed that their progress was destined to benefit them in all aspects of life. They expected that their system would always enable them to purchase whatever consumer goods they needed and to enjoy increased comfort and also provide them with efficient healthcare and that, therefore, their lives would be not only easier but longer too.

However, they never realized how wrong they were. They had managed to conquer their outer world because they had uncountable resources to invest in material things, but they had failed, through their actions, to conquer the inner world that all humans have. In conclusion, this sophisticated society gradually grew apart from Man, who had earlier been the main object of its efforts and achievements.

The fact that they could watch the sun rise everyday had made them feel proud of having a divine origin, in the belief that the great star only came out to shed its light on them and their glories.

Nevertheless, maybe because the high mountains prevented them from seeing the sun going down, these people became very superstitious, and they also acquired an apocalyptic notion of death. It is interesting to note that they used a euphemism, "the great beyond" to refer to this passing, and this is a clear indication of how far from their understanding the inevitable had become.

This fact reminded me of the sailors of old times, who were all convinced that what lay beyond the horizon was hell upon earth. Their world ended in an infernal abyss where death was certainly awaiting them.

They, like the inhabitants of the lost civilization, had not realized that the dreadful beyond was only a symbol that represented their fear to walk new paths; they were paralysed, for new roads meant that they would have to see their lives from a different place, and that they would have to acknowledge their limitations and the fact that their omnipotence was nothing but pretence.

The land was divided into carefully demarcated plots, to which their inhabitants had given the general denomination of countries, and these, in turn, had been given different names which identified them.

The different countries were governed by a ruling class, formed by a political and a religious sector, which had, in theory, been elected by their people in the first case, and by their God, or better said, the God which best suited them, in the latter. These people had always shown that they wanted to believe in their free will, even though they might have known or perceived that the people who ruled them always belonged to an elite whose members followed its guidelines and protected those who became responsible for government actions.

Those who belonged to the different sectors of the ruling class had underhandedly designed a kind of nepotism that allowed their perpetuation in power. They had conceived a new concept of family, where the bond that united them was no longer their common blood but that generated by their mutual corruption and their down and dirty actions, their ambition and greed.

They had stealthily destroyed, long before the final collapse, the original system of government of the people, by the people and for the people, such as the once conceived by Abraham Lincoln. In its place they had substituted a system where the people didn't count at all, as it had been designed for their groups and for themselves.

The members of this society, the same as those from "The Site", had different religions, which on many occasions had been used, with the support of their respective religious leaders, as an excuse to engage in atrocious wars, whose real aims were actually ignored by the public, but were justified and shown as noble and legitimate by their published opinion.

In order to suit their interests, they managed to create the most irrational and unrealistic conflict, which they explained using a pompous language, difficult to understand by the majority of the people. They spoke of clash of cultures, ethnic purification, religious wars, discrimination, famine, massive destruction weapons, global enemies, etc. The reasons to start a war were always plenty, but those to avoid it were never enough.

They hypocritically showed that they were deeply offended when someone dared to doubt the different official versions and suggested that the real causes of the conflict could be a range of possibilities, including the authorities' own actions, the natural resources of the enemy or the mere intolerance from one group to the other.

For example, if a Christian was slain by a Muslim, this private crime could result in a bloodbath, with the excuse that all Muslims were potential murderers of any followers of the Christian faith. The same happened if a Christian government started a conflict against a Muslim country. In this case, to many of the followers of Muhammad this was evident proof that all the Christians, or all those who were not members of Islam, were assassins of the Muslims, and nobody stopped to find out which was the real cause of the conflict.

What most intrigued me about all this, was reading that the religious class on each side blessed their weapons so that they would succeed in killing the enemy. I wondered whether this ritual was a kind of ordeal designed to placate their insecurities, as they probably felt how far away from God they were and in this way they would prove with their triumph which of their gods was the mightiest. No one had realized that God's battles are won without killing because they are fought within the hearts of men.

One of the things that characterized this society was the strong racism prevailing among its members, even though apparently all of them felt offended by the sole mention of this issue. No one would admit being a racist, but they all practised discrimination in some way or another, and this fact was socially accepted.

On many occasions, this racism was exteriorised openly, and at times it appeared in the form of big campaigns in aid of different racial groups or the so called minorities. This was a form of keeping them in their place, and to avoid taking serious responsibility on the part of the wealthier and more powerful groups regarding the pitiful situation of the needy. Nobody wanted to admit that the support of the increasing comfort of their own group could be one of the reasons for the decadence of the others.

On what grounds did they apply the denomination of minority to social groups which, even though belonging to a different station, or skin colour, or religious belief, were like them members of the Human Race? How could they call those groups minorities, when many times they were actual majorities that had been reduced to subjection and a state of submission by the action of those who pretended to protect them and, instead, had nearly driven them to the verge of extinction?

This was a society where the production of foodstuffs and goods was not a problem at all, whereas the problem lay in their distribution as well as in the proper allocation of resources. For example, in certain areas, the obese population exceeded that of undernourished people.

Huge budgets, condoned by silent majorities, were destined to warfare and to overfed privileged social groups. This contrasted with the scarcity of the basic minimum resources required to solve serious health and malnutrition problems, utterly ignored but profusely justified by those responsible for this state of affairs. They seemed to be completely unaware that these problems could eventually hit them too.

This could have been one of the reasons why some members of this affluent society gave so much importance to ecology and the defence of the environment; which meant spending huge sums on the protection of the endangered flora and fauna, while at the same time, turning their backs to the real problems which affected human beings from other social groups.

They never realized, not even in the midst of the disaster, that it is useless to protect a panda or a whale if the members of one's own species are not protected from any risk of extinction, especially when many of the reasons for their situation are, like in the case of the pandas or the whales, the result of human actions.

Another feature that characterised this society, which I came to know through the study of their language, was that euphemisms and doublespeak were common aspects of communication. These were frequently created and used as means to avoid calling things by their real names.

These people had not understood that the most important things are not those which are not mentioned, on the contrary, they are those which are expressed with clarity and courage, and taking the risk of the effect they will cause on those who hear them.

This peculiar way of using the language by the members of the different communities, was often the manner in which they justified themselves, either as individuals or as communities. As it also was an effective way to rid themselves of any kind of responsibilities or blame that might have corresponded to them regarding social cataclysms resulting from their actions or their lack of response to prevent them.

How could they feel responsible for things whose real magnitude or significance they had been unable to understand? How could they know or comprehend what they were being told, if the terms they had learned to define certain circumstances were not being used to communicate these facts to them?

In this omnipotent society, all the questions designed to ascertain the commitment of its members were purely rhetorical. They not only knew all the answers, but also the solutions already designed for the issues submitted to them, for they felt completely apart from any kind of responsibilities regarding these problems.

For example, in their opinion, every diplomatic or military conflict started by their government was justified stating the need to put an end to any slaughter or famine, or an alleged ethnic depuration or, why not, to stop the potential danger of a nation, which most of the times was too poor and too weak to defend itself from a country, most of the times, rich and of an overwhelming military power. Of course, these conflicts usually ended with the liberators taking possession of any strategic resources or region of the country in whose aid they had come, with the euphemistic excuse that they would manage them seeking their general welfare, but always excluding the weak nationals from this administration.

These powerful nations were in general tolerant with those who denounced what was happening. This benevolence was an outward expression of freedom, but the truth was that there was a secret strict control over all these manifestations and that it was certain that these rebels wouldn't go any further than making verbal protests to which the general public would pay little attention.

The family was one of the fundamental pillars of this society. According to the images I saw, both parents and authorities enjoyed being photographed with children of all ages.

It is amazing when one realizes that the feeling of happiness and well being shown in a photograph does not always correspond to the reality of the people portrayed in it!

Most of the children from the so called rich countries, at an early age were sent by their parents to places especially designed to receive them and where they were practically brought up by people totally alien to their families. However, in poor countries, probably due to the lack of means, many children were raised under the supervision of a member of their family.

Generally speaking, parents followed the wrong concept that they had to make whichever effort was needed to provide their children with the best possible comfort. This was the reason why they devoted most of their time to work in order to acquire goods and money, using the pretext of "self achievement" and claiming that it was better to give their children "quality time" rather than giving them "quantity time", as though there was such an abysmal difference between these two behaviours that it was impossible to implement both at the same time.

No one in this seemingly perfect society had any insight into which the children's real needs were.

Maybe some of them felt that quality of time was the quantity of time they spent with their parents, as a way of feeling protected by them, or it could just mean that they didn't want a period of time based on what their parents regarded as quality. They probably wanted their time.

This could have been one of the motives why an estrangement occurred when these children grew up and saw their parents getting older and the latter also realized they were no longer needed. Moreover, this fact might have eventually led to the constitution of families who not only ignored their origins but also the reasons for them.

There was such an obsession for the acquisition of goods, that failure to obtain those regarded as "essential" by the social environment generated serious personal conflicts that could lead to the implosion of family groups. The obtainment of goods became the only real cause which justified all kinds of efforts, to the point that many people bought things they knew they wouldn't be able to pay or that were of no real use to them, as they were also aware that their purchase also meant that they would have to work more hours, taking time off their families.

Consumption knew no boundaries. A deceptive publicity had been designed to promote the idea of personal satisfaction and social achievement by encouraging the inhabitants of the different countries to obtain whatever was offered to them. These people didn't realize that they were consuming themselves when they were extensively using non renewable resources or other materials beyond their possibilities.

Hedonism and the facile style, propelled by the ruling classes and the producers, had ousted all the other philosophic theories as role models to pursue.

Consumerism had become one of the principal silent enemies of society and the fact that it had been fostered, regardless its cost, was the hidden reason behind many conflicts and their subsequent justification, including that which led them to their obliteration.

This was a society where different medical schools, acting as corporations, fought and very scientifically disqualified each other to become the owners of the truth in respect of systems or methods to treat diseases. It was inconceivable to expect them to interact or collaborate between them in order to find a breakthrough in the search of new drugs or methods for the benefit of the health of those they were supposed to protect.

The health system was subtly controlled by the big pharmaceutical companies, which had found the legal means to sell certain medicines, which they alleged would cure diseases for which no remedy had ever been found before, when actually these drugs were either innocuous or, even worse, more harmful than the illness affecting the patient. All this was achieved not only by the unscrupulousness of certain physicians but also by the protection received from the governments.

The prevailing medical system treated separately the illnesses of the body and the soul. Albeit it had managed to cure the symptoms of many diseases, it had practically never been able to cure radically any illness, much less, the person that was ill. It was a system which, despite the supposedly huge sums of money invested, could never prevent the appearance of new diseases of unknown etiology, or originated from the mutation of viruses or bacteria that were believed to have been eradicated.

The well to do members of the affluent sector of this society had made their bodies their main object of cult and care, while they foolishly neglected their spiritual being, their inward self. That being which statistically has little value, but the one which ought to have been the ultimate aim of all human actions.

The different societies developed within this context, until due to reasons not quite known, one of the member countries, with the purpose of protecting itself from possible enemies, developed a super virus capable of eliminating the most powerful foe without giving it time to realize what was happening and defend itself.

The creation and justification of the new biological weapon became a clear example that the combination between ignorance and pride is capable of generating arms of uncontrollable massive destruction, supported by ideologies that can destroy not only its own creators but those who they want to benefit too.

The people of that old order never became conscious that the only enemy of their societies dwelt within each and every one of their members. It made them conceal their intolerance, justify the governments they had created and supported, as well as the different groups that added fuel to the flames of intolerance and used this against others with total contempt for human lives.

When one day, someone who became aware of the latent danger tried to warn the people, the authorities not only persuaded public opinion that this was just a lie invented by someone who in this way showed that he was the real danger to all of them. Moreover, he was falsely accused of consorting with possible enemies, and this fact, together with other mendacious arguments, was used to justify an arms race against any other country.

How late the man in the street realized that, when conflict is the issue, paranoids are seldom wrong.

The conflict escalated and became very serious, until one day, in the big cities, people started to die of unknown reasons, one after the other.

The powers that be gave thousands of plausible explanations in order to disguise what was actually happening. It was even suddenly stated that the plague was caused by a virus which had escaped from a military laboratory, but no one was held responsible for this.

That was the day, not any other, when all governments, fully aware of the danger threatening their people started working together, regardless race, creed, religion or ideology. But it was too late, the virus couldn't be stopped, it spread as silently, as it had been created and had arrived, killing all forms of life then known.

Only then, when they knew that their end was near, the people started asking themselves questions, searching for answers that, if found before, might have allowed them to avoid the tragedy.

It is symptomatic that many times, when we become aware of the proximity of death, as a last hope we resort to some kind of faith, and the most confirmed atheist turns into a devout believer.

Thus, every member of each community, when feeling in front of the inevitable, resigned their senseless omnipotence and asked their God, or the one they adopted for the occasion, once and again, to save them and their loved ones. It was at this crossroads in their lives, when all that was material ceased to be of value to them.

The History

If you expect different results, don't keep on doing the same thing.

ALBERT EINSTEIN

At this time, alone and refusing to be beaten, walking relentlessly towards my death, my life has come to be part of an ephemeral world and my dreams impossible. What good is it to think of my own history, or that of my people, when we are bent on looking for different alternatives to disavow or warp it?

How often have you asked me, and the dwellers of "The Site", about our history? How often have we given you a single version of it, while history, which consists of human facts, always has more than one version, and all are based on evidence that justifies them; since Man justifies everything that in one way or another benefits or damages him.

How many times have you found yourself unable to analyze recent facts, because of the simple reason of lacking objectivity due to the short time elapsed since their occurrence?

How many times have you found that those analyzing the past tampered with it once and again and finally twisted it, and, in the selfsame fashion, also altered its factual causes?

How many times and for whatever reason has hiding and denying facts, or ascribing them to others, or deforming them, or simply not wanting to make way in our quest for them, made us repeat our mistakes because we fail to recognize their real causes and consequences?

How many times have we mixed up historical exactness with ideological rigour, or religious beliefs, to make it suit our own convenience?

We have been far more steadfast in concealing the truth than in finding it and disclosing it.

We have been much more dedicated to discover objects or physical facts linked to the ends of our quest of answers, than to attempt to enter the world of passion and feeling of their protagonists.

Isn't it strange that within a society where matter has been an important component, very few have dwelt upon the reasons that made their ancestors behave in a certain way or develop certain conducts or produce certain objects?

We all know a glass was made to hold liquids, but what else made a predecessor Man invent it? Was it perhaps their need to socialize with equals that made them look for the best way to drink?

What did the murderer feel before performing the act he was compelled to do? What did the artist feel that permitted his creation? What did the scientist aim at, and what did he think that drove him on his research? What did the statesman really think that made him perform his actions?

Did no one understand it is far better to ache for the past, which is irreparable, than for the future which is in the make?

Could it be that our present is none other thing than our past? Could it be that we are just a projection of our present? Could it be that our idea of the future is just a different way in which we see ourselves? Could it be that our markedly relative vision of the past and hazy vision of the future is just an outcome of the fact that we are mere thoughts, and that these are ruled by their own direction?

How can it be that no one, despite being submerged in this tragedy, has realized that reality will eventually appear before us? Unless we denied it, confronting ourselves with our own often warped and stereotyped version of reality, would give us the chance to value that which deserves to be valued, and not to repeat those things that we would regret, because we participated in them, or because we consented them? Truth, like smoke, will sooner or later give evidence of its presence.

It is not man who stumbles twice over the same stone, which because it is inanimate does not have any responsibility in his striding, it is him who stumbles twice over himself, it is Man from the past and Man from the present who hinder themselves and crash into each other, denying themselves, without realizing they are the selfsame thing. They have not understood that, with their unconscious actions, behaving as two equivalent physical forces of same but opposing intensity, the one thing they will achieve will be to abolish their future, or rather to create an uncertain future, a fragile and unpredictable product of their shortcomings.

We have refused to see and accept that like tree roots seek for the truth of water to be able to grow up strong, and like a fish must swim against the current to be able to spawn future generations, we must behave in likewise manner, and take whatever risk is needed in our quest for truth. Haven't you realized we have always refused to know the reasons why we are where we are?

It was not important to know how we arrived; our official history would always find answers to that, some more epic than others. The important thing, which we never told you directly, was why we are here, being only present, since we deny the past and build the future with our minds and tear it down with our actions.

As a society made up of blind men, who have lost their eyesight, expanding their other senses, we refuse to feel and vibrate in an identical frequency with Nature, which does not have any other alternative than to welcome things as they come, with no conscience of the future, which is no other thing than a summation of present moments.

We have refused to accept that our permanent commitment must be with life only, which is much more than a commitment with our neighbour because it also concerns, and very especially, those who are not our fellows.

Living always requires the courage to hold on to that which we believe in, even though we know the risks which we are exposed to.

Our lack of commitment was the main reason for our misfortune. Not seeing, not speaking out, or simply not acting, were just the consequence, and later the excuse for our conduct, never its origin.

The Beginning

Anyone entrusted with power will abuse it if not also animated with the love of truth and virtue.
JEAN DE LA FONTAINE

Even though they were blind, a few inhabitants of the different regions and countries managed to escape alive from the attack by that senseless biological weapon which they had chosen not to know of, or to prevent its production, and they thanked their gods for having spared them from an inevitable death.

They never understood that it wasn't the weapons they had produced what killed the people, that the truth was that they had killed each other. They always refused to admit that not even the finest musical instrument can play a melody by itself; a weapon itself is not lethal. It was Cain's hatred, not the instrument he used, what killed Abel.

What was the use of owning so many material things, which they promptly left behind without even considering what they had meant to them? What use could they make of all the unnecessary objects they had accumulated? Where did their pride to belong somewhere suddenly go overnight?

Only the survivors remained, just thinking about saving themselves and those who they most cared for, without even considering quality or quantity of time, or goods, which are luxuries that can be afforded only by those who have never ceased to think of themselves alone.

In this state they carried on during years, marching together towards the mountains, holding hands, in columns where white, black and yellow blind men, women and children blended together, without any longer bothering about the colour of their skin or their religion. Their only aim was to get as far away as they could from the catastrophe.

They all felt like brothers suffering a common loss. They had all learned that it is impossible to help others if one has not humbly accepted being helped in one's turn.

It is amazing how pain brings us much closer than happiness or prosperity! How difficult it is to be able to realize that at times of crises, what used to be absolute becomes relative and that which used to be a priority is no longer important; what is more, we are incapable to even notice that this has ever happened!

The days passed for these living shadows of what they had once proudly been, and along the long march, people of different skin colours began to mix into the lines of the other groups. They may have done this intentionally or maybe without thinking, but the result was that they started to feel that they belonged there, even though that was not their reality.

It was in this manner, with their beliefs and misgivings that the first inhabitants arrived at "The Site". Soon, the members of the different groups once again started to distance themselves from the others. It was surprising indeed to see how men obstinately insisted on repeating the cyclical pattern of their history.

It started when some alleged spiritual guides resorted to the argument, stated in a very determined and clear manner, that it was impossible for them to worship their God in the presence of worshippers of false deities. It was their God, they said, and not any other, who had saved them from the catastrophe, without noticing that the other groups said the same regarding their respective gods, because they too believed that each of them was the real saviour.

A further disruption occurred when the leaders of the different communities, began to assign their own groups qualities that excelled those of the others and blamed the latter for the reasons for the disaster. Even though the argument they used to justify this accusation was merely emotional, they all managed to change history to their own convenience.

Once the new groups had settled down, gradually, a ruling class began to grow in them. Initially, their members were elected by the population of each group, but with the passing of time, they themselves chose those who would become rulers.

This was the dynamics of power until the day arrived when, with the excuse of avoiding possible conflicts between the groups, all the rulers of the different places decided they should meet and agree on common policies aimed at facilitating the coexistence both within and among the different groups.

These meetings went on during months without achieving any satisfactory results, until the day came when some of the leaders of several communities were found dead, and this paved the way for the consolidation in power of a new ruling class who replaced those who had died.

The same happened with religious leaders of the different creeds in "The Site". These men, to show their goodwill to find paths in common, met in a great Council, but many of them died mysteriously and, in this case too, a new religious class was born.

No one gave much importance to these deaths, which were attributed to latent sequels of the virus that had killed their families long ago, on the other side of the mountains.

Even though some of them were not satisfied with this explanation and felt there was something rather suspicious in these events, they preferred not to try to find the truth. The official version was enough for them, as long as they could avoid committing themselves to any course of action.

From then onwards, the new ruling classes, when consolidated in power, both political and religious, explained that in order to see to the collective security, they would all live together in a new settlement, which they called "The Centre", with all the other different places subjected to it.

When one is used to living with death, dying actually doesn't mean much, and that is why no one at that time wondered how it could be possible that these leaders should live under the same roof. For these were the same men that had instilled in them the feeling that they were all different, that each of their gods was the true and only, and that their group was not only better but superior than the others, etc, etc. Now, these men lived practically together, sharing identical interests.

Nobody noticed this latter fact: they were actually sharing common interests. "We" had consolidated their power through a well kept joint secret, their nearly total lack of vision and that irremediable trait of human beings that leads them to try to dominate and control the members of their own species, even at risk of repeating the history that had driven them to the verge of their total disappearance.

The ambition of "We" was as beyond measure as were their teachings to "Those from

There". They were based on a culture that feared the infringement of any regulation established by them, and always in agreement with the canon dictated by the different "only" gods to their spiritual guides, who were also a part of "We".

These teachings only served to foster both personal and collective insecurity among the different groups, which in turn contributed to the growth of fear and scorn on the part of the members of each group towards those from the others.

The lyrics of the anthem called "The Chosen Ones", that "We" made all the people of "The Site" sing, were sufficient enough to understand how powerful and evil was their subliminal technique to control and indoctrinate them.

We are "Those from There".
The ones our only God has saved.
We are the chosen from "The Site".
We are blind but
"We" look after us.
"We" were chosen by God
Nothing will happen to us due to "We"
"We", the beginning and the end.
We are the chosen from "The Site",
We, the blind looked after by "We"

As this anthem was repeatedly sung by all the inhabitants of "Those from There" from an early age, and in every group where they belonged, they all felt assured that its words were destined to their group only; that is to say, that theirs was the chosen group, and this provoked the irrational rejection of the others.

Iridescence

The only thing necessary for the triumph of evil is for good men to do nothing.
EDMUND BURKE

Just like light frequently produces changing effects on the colours of things, in likewise manner, the various experiences we undergo change their visage and acquire aspects which are diverse to their realities.

What if truth were akin to the colour of things, which only exists because of light, not by itself? What then would be the Light that would allow us to discover truth? Which truth, the Aristotelian truth, reflected in reality; the religious truth, based on dogmatic faith; or truth as a consensus between men, based on beliefs and interests?

How is it possible that we haven't realized that even though we defend truth as if it were an absolute thing, both reality and truth, in a human context are just apparent and relative? What if we also had this characteristic, and because of this, the world we have made for ourselves also had it?

How is it that we have not realized we wanted to build a world starting from an ideal, which, not being physical, real, or factual, has just been part of our fantasies?

Inadvertently, we have built a society in our image and likeness, mute, fearful, blind, and insensitive.

How can we feel any kind of emotion, save those which concern us directly, when we have lost the capability to connect to others or to the world around us?

Like blind men we have only cared for that self related world close to us. We did not realize that the same blindness which once brought us together has led us to accept all the things which would make us feel secure, even at the cost of being divided.

We have given up everything for the sake of our so called safety, forgetting it is a mere concept if we do not take an active part in the process of its creation and preservation.

So many times I did say to myself, when I became aware of my own blindness, and as a secret form of rebellion against it, "Pero, even though life and events may bring you to your knees, you should never be found on your knees"

What was the good of musing, if my thoughts never gave way to action? What is the good of worrying over what can be happening and affecting us, if we are incapable of committing ourselves to find a solution, even though we reckon we might make a mistake in the choices made towards that end?

It is very sad to realize during our fall that one has always had the chance to die standing up for an idea and not because of it.

It is of no avail to be like the waters of a river, which everyone knows will end up in the sea, or some lake, but only a few know where they come from.

If we believe ourselves to be rivers we must behave as such, being conscious we haven't been born from copious and vigorous water courses, but from a modest spring and as such, at certain times we are the cause of beauty and life... sometimes their opposite. Our fortitude will arise from merging with others, maybe coming from origins very different to our own, and accepting them as they are.

Even though our path should be straight, we must never lose the significance of our destiny, nor the meaning which we have accumulated while flowing. Many circumstances might detain our waters, even the deeds of men, this is true, but they may only stop a little, because, in one way or another, water will always seek to overcome obstacles that come up, even at the cost of having to set down a new course. The main thing is to move forward towards our fate.

How could we not realize that the foremost mission of even the simplest of things in Nature is interaction? Even the tiniest speck of dust is a part of creation, even that which we could consider "dead", like a leaf fallen from the safety of its tree, is destined to become mould.

Day and night, shape and shadow, the seasons, laughter and crying, pain and happiness, success and failure, your look and mine; everything has a reason to exist connected to the process of our creation and growth; unless we try to find other motives to exist, through reasoning, and feel special and unique, and as a consequence, find ourselves alone in the Universe, with no origin or destiny.

In order to feel special and different to everything and to all, we have, without consciously meaning or wanting to, not only denied our own existence but also the possibility of being part of the existence of others.

It has not been a force alien to ourselves who has, in one way or another, overpowered us, but ourselves who in the incapability of handling our fear, have created and condoned a system which is made-to-order. A cowardly system, fearful of whatever might manifest itself in its essential and more liberated form.

Our question should never, when looking at our life experience, be concerned with what came first, if the chicken or the egg, since anyway we would have eaten one or the other, or both.

Our search should not have started off from a question that condemned us to rack our brains to find a meaningless rhetorical answer, but from other questions that could have made us discover new paths.

If the egg was first: How should we have acted to protect it and allow it to become a chicken some day? And if it was the chicken: How should we have acted to protect it, and its eggs, to prevent its life cycle from being hindered or terminated?

It is not through a question without an answer that we can study the laws of cause and effect; since these are linked to human experience... it is through analyzing our attitude towards the issue, since we shall always be the beginning and end of our own actions.

This is why, near the end of my road, that I can't help thinking how often I tried to convey to my children and you too, that we will never live because of what we have suffered, but because of all that we do to prevent others from experiencing the same suffering.

[101]

Like the water in a river, the power of collective conscience does not arise from great watercourses, but from the joint water of its tributaries.

It is too late to answer all those questions that I felt you were making when you, in amazement, watched my fall! How could I answer that which you should answer yourself from the depths of your being?

You, who have always prided yourself on being able to perceive all that was happening around you, are the first person you should interrogate about the causes that brought us to where we are, and be humble enough to open your heart and soul to every question you make, since you will have to provide the answer to your query.

The Beginning of the End

Liberty means responsibility.
That is why most men dread it.
GEORGE BERNARD SHAW

Due to the people's passive permissiveness, the control the "We" exercised over the different groups and individuals grew stronger every day. No one had the slightest notion of what was starting to happen yet.

"Those from There", with their silence, their fear, their lack of participation, their action or inaction, had condoned the creation of a system which, with the passing of time, would first dominate them and ultimately, destroy them.

The dominating sector, as part of their doctrine of power, had persuaded the members of each group that they were part of a just society in which individual freedom was respected, as a way to achieve the common welfare.

It was in the name of that intangible "common welfare", that one of their first resolutions established that in each community a member of "We" would reside for a short period, with full powers to designate its representatives. The measure was supported by reasons related to good government, increase of individual and collective security, and as a manner of bringing power nearer the different places, increasing the participation of the people in the decision making process.

Once the civilian authority was established, the religious authority on its part, claiming that they had noticed that certain people were behaving in an improper manner, contrary to their teachings, which they had received straight from their God, condemning them both explicitly and implicitly, used this as an excuse to decide that one of its members would permanently reside in each community, to look after the health of their souls. With the agreement of the civilian power, the obligation on the part of all the population to attend their rites was enforced under threat of both earthly and divine punishment.

After the consolidation of the authorities designated in the different places, with the exception of "The Others", where only the civilian authority was accepted, the "We" created a compulsory universal system of education and a collective system of justice.

The educational system, conceived with the purpose of controlling and designed to teach not to think, would repress as dangerous any idea or behaviour that appeared to be creative or contrary to those stemming from "The Centre". Intelligence has always been the worst enemy of mediocrity.

By means of teaching, as socialization techniques, many different disciplines and only one doctrine, the educational model had been, basically, created to suppress any kind of dissent, under the excuse that the latter only served to destroy the prevailing social and religious order, which made people free.

The system's development, as well as the conduct of those appointed to teach, was permanently and closely supervised by both civilian and religious authorities.

The judicial system was organised starting with a court in each community, which was presided by a member of "We" or any other person designed by him.

This court, in the name of a supposed transparency and with the purpose of making the inhabitants of each place rest assured of the rationality of their verdicts and aiming to also make them fellow participants of their decisions, named a jury of seven members chosen at random among the residents, by a drawing mechanism which was controlled by a member of the "We".

How could one realize that having laws and enforcing them is not always a guarantee of justice? Weren't the cruellest dictators proud to show the world how in their governments all laws were obeyed, albeit these were laws dictated by them in order to ensure their power?

Lastly, with the alleged purpose of making all government acts public, "We" established that they would publish the measures taken and those to be taken in the future, with the aim of counting with the approval of most of the people of the different communities.

"Those from There", didn't understand the danger that was brewing from the concentration of power they had contributed to create. They had deposited their rights and liberties in the hands of the "We", so that they would administer them for the benefit of all.

Who wouldn't want a more efficient government? How would one oppose to being part of a society tending to be morally perfect, even more so, when this was part of the path leading to God? Who wouldn't refuse to live in a system within which law had to be respected and justice be done through its own members, as a warrant of impartiality?

How could they become aware of the fence that "We" was building to enclose their lives? How could they have an opinion on things they didn't know or couldn't prove, or didn't want to know and prove?

On many occasions, when I was speaking about these subjects with different residents of the place, about the dangers they could represent to their communities, unequivocally all of them agreed in their explanations of the great benefits that the new systems had brought to their lives and those of the other members of their group.

Pero, as well as the other people of his community, systematically always regarded all and each of my questions as coming from a person who didn't quite know either their system of life or the good intentions of the "We", in creating them. He had never analysed their feasibility at all.

They commented that their children were receiving more and supposedly better education; that the level of security in each community was undoubtedly higher because there was more vigilance in their streets and, fundamentally, that the extent of freedom enjoyed by each of the inhabitants of "The Site" would not only have been the envy of past generations but that it would possibly be their legacy to those who would come in the future.

As regards the regulations established to punish any action against the "We" or their legislation, either consciously or not, Pero was convinced that these could only mean a problem for dissidents, if there were any, in view that he and his family would never be affected by them because of the simple fact that their behaviour always agreed with the precepts dictated by the government.

Conformism had become one of the worst enemies of Pero and his community. They didn't understand that under any authoritarian system of government, to abide by the rules would not always be reason enough not to be found guilty of a crime that they might have never committed.

They didn't realise that each day there were more people sent to trial by these courts without any real cause, except that of thinking differently or refusing to condone acts or deeds contrary to their ways of thought or their ethical conception of life.

Under the mean justification that they might have done something, all the inhabitants of the different places accepted that many innocent people should be convicted under proof and evidence submitted to an indoctrinated jury, unable to verify their validity.

No one took any notice of the defendants voicing the injustice of a process staged and manipulated in order to sentence them for the mere fact that they were in disagreement of "We", or because they thought differently regarding the dogma that had been legitimated by the people.

No one noticed, or wanted to notice the mysterious disappearances of individuals or whole families, for there was collective cover up of these events.

Every artistic or cultural expression was surreptitiously controlled and qualified, both by the religious and the civilian authorities, sometimes with the purpose of instigating the public judgement of its author, who could be judged as moral, immoral, of having either good or bad taste, or being decadent, dangerous to children, and so on.

They all felt free when, in fact none of them was. They were all, one way or another, being watched and controlled by "We", through different devices designed by its members.

"Those from There" didn't understand that the size of the cage does not make a bird freer than other; the difference may be that one is aware of its captivity and the other will never be. The worst bars are invisible to our eyes.

When the madness of some of the members of a society is regarded as normal behaviour by the rest, this same madness eventually turns out to be the parameter that measures their own sanity, as well as that of all its other inhabitants.

This *mens sana*, in the name of the defence of freedom justifies the most unjustifiable means of oppression and control exercised by an active minority over the silent, passive majorities.

A sanity which, in its refusal to admit its sickness, gives the name of freedom to all that dominates it, and many times publicly condemns all that can set it free.

The system of power within "The Site" could have been defined as a totalitarian democracy, since, if everybody agreed with "We", their actions were the product of popular will, but if people didn't agree, "We" had no option but to impose their will using different arguments, most of which were only accepted by a few but, nevertheless, were tolerated in silence and, ultimately, legitimated by the majority of the population.

Unfortunately, it was impossible to maintain harmony in a society ruled by people whose lust for power never ceased to grow and had adopted a totalitarian system of government, which, even though under the form of a democracy, had none of its principles whatsoever. No one had realized that initially there appear people of a totalitarian nature and then these people, through their acts and conducts give origin and justify totalitarianism as a valid system of government.

There is nothing more corrupt than power itself, and nothing erodes more those who hold it than the conviction of one of its members that his presence is what empowers and justifies the situation in power of the rest. How is it that we can't realize that even the round tables have a head?

I never knew the moment when the members of "We" actually started to believe that they were where they were as a result of the unequivocal wish of the inhabitants of "The Site", and not as a result of their own actions.

Both their need and greed for power were so great that they had forgotten that some time ago they had killed each other to grab it, that the real reason why "The Centre" had been planned and built was to protect themselves, regardless whatever else they said. In conclusion, "We" had achieved a system of government made to their measure, counting with the acquiescence and silence of the inhabitants of "The Site".

Dictators, as well as all other mortals, have pangs of conscience which, at a certain time of their lives, demand them to seek excuses to justify themselves and their actions, but we must always bear in mind that these excuses only serve to mitigate their own remorse, because they never feel that they need to explain their actions to others. Their pride will not only prevent them from admitting their mistakes, but it will also make them lay the blame on others for all past, present and future errors.

And so it was that one day, while the people in "The Site" were living in a seemingly harmonious system, in "The Centre" began a strong argument between the religious and the political sectors, regarding which of them constituted the real support of the other.

The members of the civil sector alleged that they had been freely elected by the people of "The Site" to rule over them, while the religious sector stated and gave examples of how they had been chosen by God, or better said, their gods, for this function. What reason might have solved was prevented by pride and, therefore, a schism appeared between them, even though initially, both sectors agreed to continue living in "The Centre", but in actual separation from each other.

The civilian sector, getting ahead of the religious, promptly announced the residents of "The Site" that, as a way to increase their liberties, they had decided to establish a lay system of education, for which they could opt freely, while at the same time decreeing that they were no longer under obligation to attend religious services.

The religious sector, when they got wind of the new regulations issued by their rivals, accepted it with reservations, but at the same time condemned in the name of their gods any person that went astray from their precepts and teachings. This attitude was due to the fact that they were aware of the convenience of avoiding a direct confrontation with the civil power, and of the need to reorganise themselves, with a new strategy and tactics.

It is quite likely that this confrontation was the cause of one of the first social fractures between the different communities that constituted "The Site".

The Sun

Since a politician never believes
what he says, he is quite surprised
to be taken at his word.
CHARLES DE GAULLE

Now that my journey is over, and I can understand metaphysically, and with sharper clarity, the many reasons that underlie my life, I also realize that the hope for a better world was never lost within me, providing that we know how to summon the courage to create it.

It has not been easy to understand that our lives are the representation of the cycles of the Sun and the Moon, where light and darkness alternate during a specific length of time, holding sway over it, without this meaning predominance of one over the other. In this continuous cycle we should remember that the Sun will always have the advantage of reminding us of its presence by reflecting its light on the moon.

I still remember that almost magical moment, when conversing with her, sitting side by side on the lawn, outside our house, under a perfect, star studded summer night, I suddenly whispered, not wanting to break the spell of the moment or be overheard, "Do you know something? I'm more and more touched each day I look at the moon, because, even though she doesn't know it, each night she gives me the strength to continue on my path, despite everything else".

"Why? What special meaning does the Moon hold for you, that you suddenly say this thing using this tender tone that stirs me up without my knowing why?" she said softly, caressing my head as if to show how close she felt to me at that spiritual moment.

"Sometimes, I think", I told her, "that if we can compare oppression with the deepest, moonless nights, when we must move with the utmost care because the darkness enveloping all things obscures the vision of their outlines and our ability to recognize which are dangerous and which are not; we should also compare freedom to sunlight, which at its peak will obliterate all our shadows with its light, like those of fear and repression".

"This is why, on nights such as this", I went on saying, "when the moon is ceaselessly shining, steadily reflecting the sunlight, and in a way reminding us that it is there waiting to appear in the firmament, I know that this dark night will sooner or later vanish... that other nights may come, which will also vanish".

"Never, ever should we lose faith that a new day will surely dawn, and we should pass this certainty on to the rest, because only faith will ever grant us the strength to wait wisely and make ready to meet it on its arrival", I said as I helped her gather the mat on which we had been sitting.

You could never understand why I accepted and even defended many rules made by "We". Don't think I didn't understand; it was simply not the right moment to argue over something that could not be avoided.

It was the system created by members of "The Centre" through its unceasing preaching, which attempted, sometimes more successfully than others, to convince us that thinking of a different world was a way of ending our own existence.

Maybe you did not realize, when you more often than once, and rightfully, condemned our cowardice, that surviving the actions carried on by "We", without giving up our principles, could be a heroic act in itself.

It isn't easy nor simple to keep your head up when everything is designed to defeat you, or to suffer the pressure of power and those that in fear of it, even knowing the fairness of your actions, also blame and judge you. It is neither easy nor simple to see how your family can suffer because of your convictions, even though these are just and your family supports you.

There are times when, like a shipwrecked sailor in the midst of the sea, we can only do that which will keep us alive, even against our own principles. Sometimes we do not act well or badly, we simply do what we can.

How can I explain that patience is the last resource of the poor and oppressed, as well as ideas are their most powerful weapon?

How can I explain that to us, in those times, power lay in being able to do and not in wanting to do, and that we couldn't do anything?

Maybe you, in your efforts to find answers to everything, especially to the question of our arrival at "The Site", did not reckon that for the sake of an alleged security, after the cataclysm, we followed the ideology and behaviour code dictated by "We", slowly and silently losing our dignity in this way. Sometimes it is impossible to climb out of a pit, just because of the shame we feel for being inside it.

Many of us refused to believe what was happening, even though we knew it was possible, because of the simple reason of feeling ashamed in the face of such veiled unfairness, which we silenced and condoned.

How to avoid feeling guilty at some moment for what we have blindly refused to acknowledge, making one thousand "valid" excuses, even when seeing the evidence before our very eyes?

How could we not feel ashamed of acts or statements concocted to justify actions, which only served to humiliate us as human beings?

How could we not feel guilty for denying the sun, even though we felt its presence and warmth on our skin? The fact that we were unable to see it did not excuse us!

How could we go on living while knowing that we had denied others their human condition with our silence, letting them be subject to limitless harassment, that we would never have allowed our pets or animals to suffer, although we regard this kind to be less than ours?

Even though we didn't feel responsible for what happened in "The Site", because of conscious or unconscious ignorance of the facts or because of having believed our government, as a form of avoiding any contact with potential problems or risks, nothing will justify us before our conscience, which will sometime confront us with what possibly might have happened if we had we acted differently.

It never occurred to us that, even though one might kneel at some time in one's life, it is impossible to spend one's whole life kneeling down.

The End

That is to be wise to see not merely that which lies before your feet, but to foresee even those things which are in the womb of futurity.
TERENCE

Once a new kind of equilibrium between the two groups of power had been achieved, they set themselves to live separately, but secretly supporting each other.

They knew that any real clash between them would not only result in unforeseeable and unwanted consequences for both of them that would undermine their real power over the rest of the society.

While these events were taking place silently behind their backs, the inhabitants of "The Site" continued with their routine lives, always under the watchful sombre look of both, the religious and the civilian powers. They went on with their habit of meeting, facing the west, and hoarding the particular objects of each place; "The "Blacks", round stones, "The Whites", square ones, "The Yellows", sea snails, and "The Others", oblong pieces of wood. It was as though life was nothing else than watching time passing, just like a gentle, imperceptible breeze.

Their urge to accumulate those things which had no other value than the worth these people gave them, was so great that they had forgotten that these collections had been started by the first inhabitants of "The Site" as a simple way of keeping themselves busy while their new lives became organised.

They didn't realize that each individual's devotion to collect objects was contributing to create a completely avaricious society where its members were rewarded by the number of articles they possessed.

Maybe because this was a society constituted by blind people, they were never capable of evaluating the means used to obtain them. The important thing was to possess, the more, the better.

Therefore, as a result of this craving for possession, without asking themselves neither how nor why, nor what for, one day the members of "The Centre", who coveted the objects owned by "The Others", persuaded the inhabitants of the rest of the places that they had to stop them, so as to put an end to their claims of being different and, possibly, superior than the other communities. Emotion has always been the best ally of the mighty.

"Those enemies of the system who have no God, who feel superior for the mere fact of being physically different from the inhabitants of the other places, who have never agreed to design their houses in accordance with the pattern accepted by all the rest as being the right one, who produce their own objects and believe they are better than all the other members of the different communities, must be, once and forever, disciplined and forced to accept our system of life, with its customs and traditions, as the only true one", the civil sector proclaimed.

"We must put an end, once and for ever, said the religious sector, "to that group of atheists who offend our God. They have to be converted in order to be delivered from all evil and thus, arrive at His glory".

As a first measure, "We" established, by means of a communicate that was transmitted in a very strong tone, that for the sake of the other communities which constituted "The Site", and at the indubitable request of all its inhabitants, all the members of "The Others" should thereon:

1. Choose either the round or the square stones, or the sea snails as the only objects they would possess.
2. Hand over to "The Centre" all the wooden slats they held, as well as the tools used for their manufacture, to be deposited under the custody of "We".
3. Adopt one of the religions recognised by "We".

Obviously, all the groups, with the exception of "The Others", supported fervently the measures dictated by "We", since their rulers had persuaded them that they had acted in order to satisfy what they called the people's will.

The civilian administrator of "The Others", who was a member of, and chosen by the elite of

"The Centre", noticed the displeasure and bewilderment prevailing among "The Others" and realised that the opportunity had arrived for him to wield absolute power over this community.

So it was that he too manipulated the people's will and managed to inflame the uneasiness of the inhabitants of "The Others", and made them turn against the central power and declare their independence, naming him their sole and only ruler.

All the other people from "The Site", when learning about the defiant action of their adversaries, wondered with annoyance how these men had dared to oppose with total impunity both the "We" and the authority of "The Centre", which had been validated by the inhabitants of all the different communities. Moreover, they also asked, "How can we put up with the fact that "The Others" should segregate themselves from "The Site" and destroy this work of our ancestors, the product of their mishaps and their joint effort?"

All these questions were accompanied by furious outbursts against "The Others", fuelled by members of "We" blended into the crowd, claiming vociferously that "The Centre" should take strong measures against the rebellious transgressors.

This situation lasted for many days without "The Others" surrendering their position and, eventually, the much feared and by all desired ultimatum was issued:

"If, tomorrow, by the rising of the sun, the rebel community has not accepted unconditionally the rules dictated by "The Centre", which are the fruit of the common will of all the people that constitute "The Site", and thus, cease in their attempts at independence, and turned in their alleged leader, who has viciously altered the trust deposited in him by "We", all the other communities together, much to their sorrow, will be forced to take exemplary measures against "The Others", its inhabitants and their leader".

It was during those days when the two sectors taught their people a new word, which was emotionally strong, but void of content. They all resorted to the term "Honour" to justify what reason could no longer explain.

Both the pride of "The Others" and the decision made by "The Centre" were considered by the respective sides as an affront to their honour. All the parts involved in this affair claimed to be constituted by honourable men, and by alleging this they justified what was to come, including death.

No one stopped, not even for a second, to consider which their options were when they had to choose between honour and life, between honour and family, or between honour and love.

I was truly upset when the new day arrived and I noticed that the leaders of both sides were not only completely adamant but were deploying their people, with the blessing of their respective religious authorities, with the intention of destroying their opponent.

As a consequence, in the belief that they were doing the right, fair and noble thing, people who had once been sensible, turned their tools into weapons and irrationally started killing each other, for the glory of all, the power of a few and to no one's benefit in the end.

Once "The Others" had been eliminated, their leader was seized and made to walk along all the victorious places. Subsequently, to show that he was an example not to be followed, and to the people's rejoicing, he was brought to public trial, which appeared to be just and impartial. He was sentenced and mercilessly executed for having subverted the order, with the approval of many and the silence of a few. His remains were cremated and his ashes thrown to the sea, so that no trace of him would remind people of his presence in "The Site".

In order to compensate the ambition and the effort of the victors, after having wiped out all traces of "The Others" from the face of the earth and, maybe as a form of throwing a veil over their common shame, all the belongings of the defeated were distributed among the people of the different communities, with the exception of the little wooden boards, which were confiscated and deposited in "The Centre" under custody of "We".

When the conflict was over, there were days of celebrations in all the different places, which were encouraged by the central power, as well as religious ceremonies, full of pomp, to give thanks to the god of each community for having allowed them to defeat their enemy. An enemy who had never been given the opportunity to defend itself against its own external or, much less, its internal, enemies.

During those times, the inhabitants of each place, both individually and collectively, boasted their heroic deeds and bravery, which, according to them had been crucial in the achievement of the final victory. They also regarded this as the certain evidence of the superiority of their group over the others. It was not enough for them that they had annihilated the enemy, they also needed to destroy themselves!

Once peace was restored in "The Site", "Those from There" were no longer the same. Even though they didn't mean to, the day they had killed "The Others", they had also killed themselves and, especially, their feeling of security.

It may be a form of divine *quid pro quo*, the fact that no one can forget death after having faced it, nor the different sounds, smells or fears that come with it. This fact may be justified in many ways, but death, from that day, and forever, will remain alongside us on the path of life.

It was for all these reasons that each and every member of "We" began to suspect the others' attitudes, and this made the sensation of insecurity and conspiracy among its dwellers the only authentic thing within "The Centre" A sensation that contributed to unbalance the more than unstable equilibrium that had existed there.

The fear of their respective inhabitants resulted in the enclosure of the communities behind tall fences, which were carefully guarded. What is more, no one except the residents of the place was allowed in, unless being provided with the corresponding authorization.

Although the members of each community proceeded with their custom of meeting at twilight time, they had put bolts and latches on doors and windows to protect their homes whenever they went out of them. They were no longer sure of their neighbours' intentions. They no longer felt sure of theirs either.

As time passed, the situation in "The Centre" got worse each day, until it became unbearable to its members. Therefore, once again resorting to the excuse of decentralization and democratization of power, they made the decision to abandon the place and move to their respective places of origin, and destroyed it completely.

When both, the civilian and the religious rulers, moved to their own communities, they immediately set themselves to build up their power in these places. To this purpose, they fortified them, they reinforced the existing fences; they also increased the internal security measures and the control over the population. They also built different kinds of weapons and trained the residents under a pseudo military discipline, alleging that they had to prevent any attempt, either from outside or inside, that might endanger their religion and way of living.

Different objects were created, which not only served to identify them as a group, but also the sole mention of any of them served to unite their people into one for the sake of any spurious interest invoked by their leaders.

The religious sector supported these events and blessed the new custodians of the place, as well as their old and new weapons. They preached that the people should feel protected by a real God, which was obviously their God, against the heretics. "You have been chosen by Him", they said, "to end with paganism, and with the false gods of the other groups. Do not fear, because when the day of the battle comes, God will be on your side, next to you, fighting with you".

By this time, no one had any recollection that when God gave Moses the Commandments, He stated "Thou shalt not kill", and that there were no exceptions or justifications for this, not even those made in His own name.

Periodically, the official spokesmen not only highlighted the qualities of the people of the place, many of them non-existent, but also debased those of the inhabitants of the other communities, whom now they contemptuously called "strangers". To make matters worse, they had distorted the causes and the history of how the first settlers had arrived at "The Site".

All of them exalted the superiority of the race to which they supposed to belong and which was the origin of the names of the places they inhabited. All of them exalted their own and only god, the one who had spared them from the catastrophe because they were the chosen ones.

Once again, they all spoke about the Honour of being and the Honour of belonging. Once again, they all spoke about their insecurities.

It can be said that, with the passing of time, slowly but inexorably, like in a self fulfilling prophesy, everything seemed to be arranged for the inevitable. There was nothing to do but wait, like in Cassandra's myth, for things to happen.

They came to the absurd of giving the name of barbarians to those who not long ago had been considered their neighbours in "The Site", like the ancient Greek had done in their times with all those who were alien to them. But in this case, these people, like them, descended from a common misery and from individual pain.

¿How could I remain impassive and indifferent to what I was witnessing and also foreseeing what was going to happen, without its protagonists willing it? I didn't resign myself to the role of spectator of the future events I was certain would occur, especially because I was also aware that the inhabitants of the different places would eventually unleash their human nature and their folly would lead to the repetition of the awful events that had brought them to "The Site".

"You can allow yourself many things in life, but there is one we cannot allow ourselves ever, that is, to remain impervious to the pain and miseries of others!

It is also true that at times of great risk, danger or distress we find ourselves full of a special energy that we had never suspected we had. When I found myself in that amazing condition, I gathered all the notes I had made and the documents I had collected during my stay there and started a frantic search for Pero.

I hoped to give him all this information I had in my power, which not only proved the origins of "The Site" and its first inhabitants, but also the events that had led to the catastrophe, and that Pero would become the giver of all this knowledge to the other people in his community and thus the forthcoming events might be prevented.

Eventually, I learned that Pero, like many other people, at that time was attending a religious meeting of his cult, to ask their god to save them from the attack of their supposed enemies and to give "The Whites" the necessary strength to destroy them.

All the communities had lately humanized their deities to such extent that, without consciously intending it, they changed a merciful God of peace into one that was revengeful and warlike. This was probably due to the need to justify in His name the deaths that their actions would bring about.

How easy it is for us to bestow upon God the most characteristic of human traits, and refuse to recognize his divinity, as a way to justify our deeds, which are often infamous!

When I found him, I slowly got to his side and called his name in a low, soft tone, but sufficiently clear for him to recognize my voice. I grabbed his arm to make him feel my urgency and the seriousness of the issue that had brought me to that place, so sacred to him.

However, he didn't understand what I had tried to convey and walked with me to his house in complete silence. As soon as we went in, using a tone of voice which made his great annoyance and disgust quite evident, he enquired about the important reason that had led me to drive him away from his god in such grave occasion.

I have never been able to understand why it is that so many people can find an omnipresent God in just one certain place only, and speak to Him from outside their own hearts.

I began my explanation, first showing my uneasiness over what had happened before and what was going on at that moment, and then started to speak about all my studies and findings.

I told him how the first inhabitants had arrived at "The Site", how the ambition prevailing in the civilization that had once existed on the other side of the mountains led those people to destroy their enemies, and at the same time causing their own disappearance.

I introduced him to my theory regarding how the different groups that were escaping the catastrophe had, inadvertently, mixed with each other. I tried to make him face the fact that all these places, now so proud to belong to a certain pure race, actually were inhabited heterogeneously by people who had lived together with the predominating race since the beginnings of "The Site".

As though nothing I was saying was really astonishing or upsetting to him, Pero interrupted me at that point to ask what had made me feel such interest in their origins.

I must confess that I was completely taken aback by his question. However, I answered candidly, and told him that since the first day of my arrival at "The Site", I had been puzzled to find white people that called themselves "Blacks", or "Yellows" or "Others"; blacks named "Whites" or "Yellows or "Others"; and yellows who defined themselves as "Blacks", "Whites" or "Others". I added that such was the fact that had aroused my curiosity to find the causes and the reasons for such odd behaviour.

I explained that, even before my arrival at "The Site", I had always thought that there was no real cause to prevent different racial groups from living together in harmony. I also commented that the assumption that one race or one human group is superior or better than any other one, was a great meaningless lie without any reason that justified it. "Pero", I said to confirm my opinion, "the difference only lies in the possibilities that people have to reach the food they need, the healthcare they need, the education they need, and so on."

"Those from There" had shown me through their actions, that only prejudice and fear of anything that was different, of not being what they think they were, was what actually made them add a false extra value to their appearance. At the same time, they looked down on those who didn't share in them, and expressed theories without any bases to support these fears and false concepts.

The blind in "The Site" had made it evident to me that if it were impossible to see and tell the colour of our skin from that of others, this colour would become irrelevant to us. Maybe this was the reason for their obsession to ask about the race of their interlocutor.

"Pero, what colour is God's skin?" I asked, with the intention of making him reflect on what I was saying.

"Go on, please, go on!" He replied, showing a mixture of anxiety and fear when I stood silent, waiting for his answer or reaction and thus creating an expectant hush.

I then said that it was really difficult for me to comprehend why, if all the people in "The Site" supposedly believed in one God, they had not realised His principles had been tampered with and turned into political issues by the ruling classes with the aim of dividing and splitting them according to various religions of doubtful origin.

That it was that selfsame ruling class, on whom they entrusted their Faith, respectable at first and later greedy for power, who had led them towards a new type of monotheistic paganism, based, not on the existence of various gods to worship, but manifold versions of the same god.

That they had been dominated by them during a very long time through precepts supposedly issued from their god, while these had really been created by their members as a form of controlling their consciences.

All this having been said, I gathered my strength and said seriously and with certainty, "Pero, I know what is the best kept secret of the members of "We".

That was the first time I saw him get really nervous, walking up and down as if something terrible were about to happen, until he asked me defiantly,

"What do you know that we don't?", "What can a foreigner know that "Those from There" ignore?".

"It is a lie that they are blind, they see!" I answered, "Even though they only make out shadows; even surrounded by them, they have the ability to see and silently control the blind men of "The Site".

"Of course, they must have told you that". "What could you know about that!? These are just the fantasies of someone who intends to confuse me. Don't you think we have enough to worry about already?" he rapped at me, with a nervous laugh.

I pressed him on with my asseverations, telling him why I knew about their non-blindness, of how I had seen them one day, going through my notes, an unheard of action for a totally blind person.

Preventing me from going on, he pushed me harshly to the farthest corner of the house, far from any outlet through which someone could have heard me.

At first I was shocked thinking he was doing this because he regarded me as dangerous because of my disclosures, as an enemy would be seen, but I finally understood by his actions and gestures that not only was he protecting me, but even more, Pero had somehow known or perceived this secret before.

When I asked him point blank if he knew something about it, after a few minutes thought he said, firmly, "Yes!, I've known this for a very, very long time".

At first, I thought he spoke figuratively but his fear of being overheard made me understand that it was more than that, and it was then that a creepy feeling, difficult to describe and forget, ran through my body.

After a prolonged silence, probably terrifying to both of us, Pero, sitting in front of me, took my hands in his, and in an extremely low voice confessed his secret with great fear; he too could see!

He told me how his parents, for some strange reason had, after years of blindness, recovered their eyesight. This ability had permitted them to silently witness some of the many killings perpetrated by their rulers, and the tremendous persecutions launched against those that for one reason or another had been considered a threat to their power, under the often conniving, silent and passive presence of the inhabitants of "The Site".

The indifference of the rest of the people and the fear and anguish provoked in them by what they saw were so great, that they vowed never to reveal their secret, and keep on living as blind people to protect themselves.

When he was born, he was born blind, to his parents' ironical happiness, who preferred him handicapped to potentially being murdered by the regime in power.

Pero told me how his father and mother had taught him to live as a non-seeing person, they themselves acting as though they were blind before him and the rest of the people, thus peculiarly hiding their abilities.

His life went on in this way until one day, to his parents' horror, who feared the worst, without himself knowing why, he also recovered his eyesight. It was then that they revealed what had been hidden from him for so long, and made him promise never, under any circumstance, to reveal what from that moment on became a family secret.

And this was how he also learnt, while being able to see, to go on living as a blind man, to speak of the things that they spoke about and, like his parents did with him, he educated his own children under the same pretence. But during that time he understood that there are things harsher and more defiling than exile and censorship: self-exile and self-censorship.

Brought together by our shared secrets, and thanking each other for the trust that we had reciprocally conferred upon each other, Pero confessed regretfully that there was nothing he could do to prevent the massacres that he supposed would unavoidably ensue.

Maybe because of that absurd reason that the ethically-minded always possess, which makes them an easy prey for the unscrupulous, Pero was resigned to die heroically, like all cowards that overcome their cowardice, in the defence of his family and community, as a way of honouring his life.

When I tried to make him to avoid the fate which he already considered inexorable, he retorted firmly, by way of closure to our conversation: "It is my destiny!" How could I make him see that often, what we call destiny is none other than a decision taken from among many different options?

The Storm

Evil resides only in your mind, not in the outside world. A pure mind will only see goodness in everything, but an evil mind will busy itself in the invention of evil.
JOHANN WOLFGANG GOETHE

All in our lives may pass. Maybe that which we have at one time despised, will surprise us at another, for being accepted and justified. The one thing we mustn't allow ourselves is to go astray from our way towards the ultimate ends of our actions; since there are a few things we can grow accustomed to as quickly in life as evil. Do you know why? Because when we don't rebel against it, somehow we consent to its rise and domination over everything it encounters, including our own lives.

As I said to you once, I have always believed that the quest for Happiness is what justifies that at certain times we have to pursue activities or consent certain behaviours, which will at other times enable us to enjoy such things that favour a pleasurable reunion with our inner selves.

You well know, since we have spent long hours discussing over it, that being happy is to me not only a right, but a duty we owe to ourselves and to our fellow beings. Otherwise, what is the good of possessing what you have or investing your energy on anything which will not lead to it?

The fact that everyone collects something or other in "The Site", or do this or that, does not mean that I should do so myself. I have always respected those who put or have put, all their energy into such an occupation, what's more, I have many times performed it next to them, but this does not mean that I share the beliefs that justify these habits.

Is the accumulation of certain goods by any chance a show of superiority? What is implicated in its gathering and storage? If others didn't bestow such importance on the said objects, would the effort be worth it? And if so, what would be the amount collected that would permit us to live happily? Which would be the out of bounds zone where we would be collecting more than we needed, with the only objective of feeling successful within a society whose members can never tell who is and who isn't a winner?

I still remember the times when "We" would in one way or another endeavour to find out how much had been gathered by other communities, knowing that these were useless, save as a display of power.

It was the race of desiring to possess as much as possible, no matter how that would condition our lives or whether it would really allow us to do what we yearned for in terms of real happiness. It was this race what brought us to consider a possible competitor collector, an enemy. Why? Because we both wanted the same thing.

How strangely do we sometimes wield the concept of equality! We are capable of fighting for it whenever we are affected when we feel excluded from a benefit, while we are just as capable of fighting with the same intensity to prevent "other equals" from obtaining the same benefits to which they have the same rights.

We have never recognized our neighbours as equals, just as fellows, they can resemble us but they should never have our same rights, albeit we announce this rhetorically.

I can still remember your smile when I said of our leaders, "There you see them, all seated at a round table as a demonstration of equality, but they all well know in which part of the circle sits the one who really controls the various mechanisms of power. To him, all the rest are equal but different from him, because he knows he must at all time show the others where the real power lies; to the rest he is an equal, because they all crave to take his place and to have the power he has over them".

In other words, we all feel equal in respect to our capacity to wield power, but not equal as regards the disposition towards sharing its benefits. Likewise, in an equilateral triangle, all its angles are equal but there is one which is positioned at the top.

Ambition and desire to possess have gradually prevented us from appraising our efforts regarding the attainment of spiritual values, in favour of gauging our capacity to accumulate material things.

That common way of thinking was what made us one day desire to have that which another possessed and we did not own.

That way of thinking was what led us to disregard, and to justify, the means with which the desired things were obtained. You were only successful through the possession or control of something.

And it was that way of thinking which made us "see" as something reasonable, things which we would have never accepted, because they caused us harm; and which drove us blindly into a conflict of an uncertain nature and an unnatural outcome.

How can we regard as an enemy someone who was my friend or neighbour a moment ago, when I didn't mind his or my origin, beliefs, wealth, religion, race, etc, etc, which are elements alien to our inner selves?

Like in the Greek theatre, one day we abruptly showed ourselves just like we were, taking off our masks and displaying our inner selves and our "model" for peace. "Those from There" were pacifists because of circumstance, not because of conviction!

How could you think that I refused to accept what was to come? Didn't you realize that many times, as if in a storm, we are only left with the ability to protect ourselves, doing whatever we can to shield us from its fury?

How often have we seen how the storm gathered in the distance and came towards us? How often have we discussed with our fellows those signs that announced some climatic disturbance of uncertain consequences to our property and family?

Do you think that if we had had within our reach the means or resources with which we could have avoided, what was forthcoming, we would not have used them? How could we not have warned others about it, and of its consequences, if we had gathered courage to do it?

Every potential catastrophe that we are able to forecast imposes upon us two obligations, a moral one and a material one; towards our fellows, to warn and help them in the crisis; and toward our families, to protect and provide them with emotional support.

Likewise, what other resource is left to men involved in a war, than to take part in it in some way, despite being against it, and make the greatest effort to avoid being harmed by his foe, or lessen the damage that may be inflicted on his land, property and family?

How can we not realize that in warfare, between the parties involved, there are no winners, just losers and that the so called wheel of history will only overturn the contenders, crushing them, in one way or another?

How could you think that I did not realize that whatever is attained through violence and force, will always require these two to be sustained and justified?

You could not understand that when I said I knew what my destiny was, I was signifying that I knew where I should have to stand to defend my family, not in order to fight for some ideology or group of power, but to protect my family and property.

I can still remember my wife's face when I informed her of my decision to fight. She just looked into my eyes resignedly, knowing there was no other option, only asking, by way of sole commentary, if I knew the time when I should leave.

How could I tell her, that if I left it was only because of my desire to remain? How could I explain to my children that this action did not imply the support of a certain system or authority, but that I was trying to prevent worse misfortunes from befalling us?

How could I show them that my fear to die had made me lose all the fear I had for the members of "We"?

I still remember a poem my father received in turn from his father, which was later engraved with a knife on a simple block of wood; perhaps at the time of the calamity or perhaps earlier:

Never forget,
That even in the deserts
With the most barren appearance
There's life... and a flower.
That we of Nature are a part,
That we are happiness and pain.
Don't let death
Arrest your stride,
Or a tyrant enslave you.
Nothing will detain your world
As long as you stand tall and walk through it!

How could I forget hearing him recite it to me once and again, in a soft voice, but gripped by the words, as though he knew that maybe, at some time in my life, that future would arrive?

How could I understand his pain from afar? How could he avoid the anxiety of knowing that his son would possibly suffer all that he had always tried to spare him from?

I can still recall how, in silence, under the sadly attentive gaze of my wife and children, I packed my things, several of them with their help, as if they were telling me: "We will always be with you... even at this time".

It is impossible not to remember the moment when I bid each one of them farewell, strongly embracing them during a few eternal seconds, without voicing my inner conviction that a warrior's natural fate is death.

That was the reason why, while I was kissing each of them, I inhaled deeply, retaining as long as possible the scent of their hair, of their skin, in an effort to leave them the best possible memory of me. I was so wrong!

During that prolonged farewell she gave me a carefully folded slip of paper, while she held my hand and suppressed her sobs bearing the warmest strained smile and the saddest looking eyes; as if to share the most intimate secret.

I could never tell her how I had silently cried that day, as I walked away from my home reading the poem she had written for me the night before... probably also in tears; heavy with the near certainty that this had been the last time we would see each other.

Maybe she already knew, as if an omen had been announced, what destiny the future that lay ahead had in stock for us both.

When words have died down;
When only silence remains;
When hands
No longer seek bodies;
When the eyes and a kiss
Become just eyes and kiss;
When the other's laughter becomes just a
grimace;
When the word far
No longer bears meaning;
When men are only remembrance;
When verse is transformed into prose;
When the future becomes the past;
And the past just the feeling of a dream;
Even then I will still love you,
Voicing silently your name.

The Apocalypse

It is said that history repeats itself,
but what is certain is that no profit
is derived from its lessons.
CAMILE SÉE

As hours passed, tension grew among the inhabitants of the different regions, always instigated by their rulers, and their fears and insecurities also increased as time went by.

By this time, no one in "The Site" had enough peace of mind to understand that their aggressive displays were not merely a reaction originated in their incapacity and the inability of their rulers to show rationally the truthfulness and legitimacy of their assertions. They were also the product of the impotence they felt because they were not able to comprehend how things had gone so far, and out of their control. Violence is always inversely proportional to reason.

It was during those times, maybe as a bad omen, that all the beasts that inhabited "The Site" suddenly disappeared. The wild animals felt what was coming and, frightened by the ferocity outleashed by the humans, ran away to be out of danger from them, but also not to be taken as any of them. It is not a trait of fierce beasts to plan the slaughter of members of their own species.

Even the moon and the stars withdrew from the skies, there being no apparent reason for this to happen. Such were the shame and disgust they felt, knowing they were shining on murderers who, in their turn, had denied them their light. No one wanted to witness such madness.

That morning, when the people living in "The Whites" saw the first columns of dark smoke rising in the north, coming from the place inhabited by "The Blacks", they were completely hushed for a long while, and then gathered with their families. They all understood that from that moment onwards there was no way to avoid what there was to come.

Even though there were already unequivocal signs that the war between the communities in "The Site" had already started, no one could imagine how it would end, or when they would actually be involved in it.

The families took shelter inside their houses, and all those who were in a position to guarantee the safety of the place, be it man or woman, young or old, were summoned by the civil power with the sound of big drums, while the religious authorities blessed them and blessed their weapons as well, once and again.

A group of volunteer scouts was promptly sent to find out about the events in the north. They returned that same day, sheltered by the shadows of the night. It was impossible for them to conceal the horror on their faces for what they had seen and heard.

These men, distraught by what they had witnessed, reported that "The Yellows", the most numerous group in "The Site", which during the period previous to the conflict had also become one of the most bellicose, had attacked "The Blacks" by surprise. The latter, unable to defend their walls had retreated to the centre of their place and had made their stronghold there.

None of them could give an estimate of the number of casualties; all they could say was that it was huge, without distinction of age or sex.

The feeling of impotence and fear of what was happening, together with the fury against the ignoble attackers, added fuel to the grudge of "The Whites" against "The Yellows". They hadn't realised that the conflict had started long before this attack, and that "The Yellows" had only had a headstart over the other communities by being the first ones in pulling the trigger. Nobody remembers how wars begin, but everybody remembers who takes the initial step!

The day after the hostilities had broken out a small delegation from "The Blacks" arrived unexpectedly at the place to the surprise of its inhabitants, and requested an urgent meeting with the powers that be, which was granted without delay.

To my surprise, as silent witness of what was happening, I heard how, resorting to arguments relevant to those things that united them, which were the same as those that once had been the reason for their irreconcilable differences, they now were asking "The Whites" to come promptly to their aid.

The religion of a group was no longer the only true one, there was just a God common to a culture that they named "Black-White". Added to this, the objects they collected were no longer evidence of their superiority, they were merely a way to identify them and to prevent being taken for members of other groups.

Their fear that it was likely that they would be destroyed by the conflict that their irresponsible ambition had contributed to create, had brought back to both groups the rationality they had lacked to avoid it.

The inhabitants of "The Whites" were persuaded by their rulers that the best way to defend themselves was to attack the locality of "The Yellows", as a preventive measure, taking advantage of the fact that the latter were fighting at "The Blacks". To this effect, they fell on the place, and mercilessly slaughtered everyone and each form of life they found on their way. Nothing could stop them.

After hours of bloody warfare, everything became turmoil, the only things that remained clear were the slaughter and the scorn felt by those called humans. It was not a group killing another; these were men killing each other.

I have never seen such butchering in the name of Peace. Neither have I been able to understand how a peace could be built over all those dead bodies without the survivors feeling a deep grudge against their living enemies.

I wondered how it was possible that people who feared their God, who loved their families, and cherished life and peace, had heedlessly broken His commandments, destroyed families in cold blood, forgotten the meaning of the word *peace* and, much worse, the meaning of Life.

When the inhabitants of "The Yellows" learned from their messengers what had happened in their place and what had been inflicted on their families, not only their hatred of the other groups billowed, but they used it as an excuse to obliterate without mercy everything they found on their way.

While they proceeded with the massacre they had started at "The Blacks", a group of "The Yellows" swiftly set off to defend what was left of their people and their homes. This caused "The Whites" to speedily withdraw, and seek refuge behind their own defences.

There are no words to describe what they found in their place, but it is ironic that they didn't realize that shortly before, they had been doing the same monstrosities to the inhabitants of the other community. They were faced with fire, fretting and floods of tears. The survivors were only capable of feeling hate when they found their lifeless families.

To finish what they had started at "The Blacks", "The Yellows" first killed mercilessly each and all the members of that community and then set fire to all its buildings.

Furthermore, in an extreme act of cruelty and barbarism, and as a sample of what awaited their enemies, they quartered those Whites they captured in their city, when they were still alive, amidst cries of hatred and revenge, and then threw them to the flames. It was like being in the presence of the devil incarnate in his much-dreaded realms.

The aftermath of these events, was of three days and nights, where sepulchral silence reigned, that served to bury and mourn the dead and to prepare for one's own demise. They all knew that the end was now inevitable.

"The Yellows" used this time to re-group themselves, rest and coldly plan their revenge. Even though they knew that they outnumbered their enemies, they were also aware that the fighting had weakened their resources, both human and material.

"The Whites" were not deceived by the apparent respite; they knew that their attack was imminent, so they reinforced their walls and carefully prepared their defence. As they could realize that they had no strength to face the enemy on open ground, they decided to wait and resist their charge, with the aim of tiring and wearing them down, and then counter attack, to eventually negotiate some kind of peace.

During all this time, Pero confidently commented that their leaders had studied and found the way to destroy their attackers with one blow, if need be.

When the third day arrived, not even the sun felt like watching what was going to happen, and hid, using the excuse of an eclipse.

In the early hours of the morning someone came running into the fortified perimeter of the place, shouting the advice that "The Yellows" were advancing towards them, with the purpose of isolating the place and destroy its inhabitants, in revenge of what the latter had done to their community.

Instantly, from a safe place, the leaders of "The Whites" gave the corresponding instructions. Namely, those who were not in a position to fight were to be taken into fortified buildings located in the centre of the city, from which, if the case needed it, the final battle would take place. A first group of combatants was destined exclusively to defend the walls; a second one, with great capacity of mobilisation, had to be ready to reinforce the points that were giving in; while a third group had to stand by awaiting orders to put into practice a secret plan, regarded as the final solution in case the other measures failed. It would destroy the enemy and save "The Whites" from destruction.

I am not going to narrate in detail what I saw, because it was such a display of disgrace and decadence. I cannot recall it without feeling degraded for belonging to a species that, on the one hand has always regarded itself as being superior to animals, and on the other, is capable of performing such savageries against its own brothers in kind, that not even the wildest beasts would have ever dared to commit. My feeling of shame is so great that I will just limit myself to give a general outlook of the events.

"The Yellows", after having isolated "The Whites", launched a cruel attack against the place. They spared neither material nor human resources to destroy the walls that protected them and kill whoever confronted them or tried to hide from them.

Henceforward, they fell on the different fortified points within the walls, and when repelled, they insisted on their attack, once and again.

After a succession of attacks and counter attacks, and near midday, "The Yellows" were forced to withdraw from the boundaries of the place, but they managed to gather their forces once more.

Their increased fury caused them to launch a further attack; with greater fearlessness they penetrated the city in the early afternoon and destroyed all its defences. Such was the force of their assault that nothing could stop them. By this time, "The Whites" had become just a wasted parody of what they had claimed to be.

However, as a final act of bravery, or despair, they closed ranks and forced their attackers to retreat outside their city, leaving a few groups within its walls.

Later that same day, when the sun was setting, led by the syncopated rhythm of huge drums, the group that had been appointed to the ultimate defence surreptitiously left the city. Taking advantage of the fact that the wind favoured their plan, they set fire to the woods that surrounded the campsite of "The Yellows" without hesitation.

However, when they heard the harrowing screams of the, until then, proud and victorious foes; when they saw these men dying suffocated by the smoke or consumed by the flames, the "Whites" were horrified. This feeling grew even more when they realised that, exceptionally, the wind changed direction and drew the fire they had started against the place they had intended to protect with it. Nature always takes its revenge on those actions man takes to use it arbitrarily to his sole benefit.

Then, the fire surrounded, and eventually spread all over the city, thus achieving what its enemies had not been able to consummate, since it totally destroyed the moral of its inhabitants, together with their homes and their families.

All that once had constituted the pride and glory of both groups no longer existed. Their sites, their woods, their homes, their families, their dreams, all were gone. In both communities, where not long ago nothing but their respective superiority was proudly claimed, now one could only see devastated people wandering aimlessly and without purpose.

Everything was covered by smoke and ashes, including their tragicomic sense of honour.

As a symbol that purifies everything, the fire did what men had not been able to do, it put an end to the conflict and made the leaders of the different groups meet to try and reach an urgent peace.

In the small hours of the morning, the survivors of both sides were informed that an agreement had been signed, which stated that there was no winner and that each part would pay homage to the bravery of the other. In this manner, the honour of the sectors involved would be preserved. There is nothing more useful than meaningless terms to justify an irrational behaviour.

One cannot assume to be a person of honour if one has not had an ethical behaviour. One cannot assume to behave ethically if one's actions don't prove it. Otherwise, all this becomes a great lie that can, not only lead us to make terrible mistakes, but what is much worse, turn us through our actions into extremely dangerous beings.

In view of the pain they had suffered, the people of both communities immediately started to celebrate this peace with great festivities where they all mixed, wishing to leave behind all their miseries.

Fate many times plays dice with us, and sometimes we fall on the wrong place and at the wrong time. This is what happened to Pero. When he saw that all he had once promised to defend had disappeared, for his family had been slaughtered, and all that he owned had been destroyed, he was bent down by sorrow and decided to leave the city without delay.

He was on his way when, by chance, he became the involuntary witness of the peace meeting of the leaders of both communities. To his amazement he overheard how, as the first topic of their agenda, they were discussing how they would divide the lands of "The Site" and the possessions of the defeated. Only when this issue had been settled, they started to speak about laying down their arms. Then, brokenheartedly, Pero also heard how the peace terms were drawn in order to protect these men's power over the different people they had driven to wage war, and that they now scorned.

Unfortunately, Pero was discovered and had no option but to disclose his capacity to see to avoid being captured. The possession of this precious sense now had turned him into an unfathomable danger for the corrupted power.

There is no worse feeling for a traitor than that coming from learning that he has been found. It was this fear what drove both leaders to make the decision that Pero should be chased relentlessly and eliminated. They wouldn't leave alive someone who had not only been a witness to their pact, but whom also had the gift of sight, and this made him an enemy too difficult to control.

Pero managed to hide for a few hours, until he realised that he would not succeed in becoming a permanent fugitive because of these men's implacable hunting for him. That evening he made up his mind: only he would be the protagonist of his end, he would choose when and how to die, and not those who were after him. In the meantime, the people, unaware of what was happening, carried on with their celebrations.

He climbed up the tallest tower of the city that remained erect, carrying in his arms the dead body of one of his children, those he had loved so dearly and those for whom he had fought, despite knowing how useless and unjustified the conflict was. From this height he shouted as loudly as he could, so that everyone should hear, what he had involuntarily seen and heard, and thus unmasking the men who pretended to be the people's saviours.

Pero, in tears, while his enemies were running up the stairs to arrest him and silence him, accused all those present, stating that all of them, like him, were part of a society of blind men without course. He added that their lack of commitment, their actions and inaction, had assassinated their own future and, to give a clear example of this, he raised his child's body several times, as an evidence of the awful consequence of what he had done, or avoided doing, for all the rest to see.

When he finished saying what he was trying to convey to his fellow men, he stopped shouting and continued speaking, like reciting, in a clear and serene way, but this time he was heard only by those who were near, and started muttering. Then, he jumped, still holding his child, and died in his fall.

The manner in which Pero chose to put an end to his life, may have been regarded by many as an altruistic form of suicide, while others might have seen it as the product of his own despair. The answer to this is not for us to tell.

At that time I couldn't hear, much less understand, what he was saying. I could only see how those who heard him stopped rejoicing and their countenances became serious. While they whispered with each other, they started holding hands, without minding with whom, without caring where they came from, what their creed or their colour were. Then, they raised their heads towards the sky, as if they were asking for deliverance for what they had known and had silenced, and their secret was revealed.

All of them, like Pero, at some time in their lives had recovered their vision and, like Pero's parents as well as him, had chosen to conceal this fact for fear of being eliminated by their rulers, without taking into account how many they were, what their strength was and how little the men that wielded power could see.

The fear that the members of the various, small and almost blind ruling classes had managed to impose over the people reminded me of some elephant trainers. Many times, when these animals are still small, these trainers tether them to a post, from which the elephant cannot get away. In this manner, when the animal grows up, the memory of this impossibility stays on its mind and they always feel the rope around their legs.

All these people, without exception, had the necessary skills that enabled them to proceed at an opportune moment in order to prevent or correct the events that had occurred. However, for the sake of their security, they chose not to see them, not to say anything and to continue pretending they were blind for fear of acknowledging what they could see or of what could happen to them if they didn't remain silent.

They didn't realise, or they refused to admit, that showing indifference to events or injustice was no guarantee that they would be spared by the power that generated them. They were blind to hatred, discrimination and death and, like the blind, they allowed to be led, even though they were totally capable to steer their own course. They were the worst kind of blind . . . those who refuse to see.

It was that night, then, when for the first time the moon and the stars showed themselves again in the sky, that they all decided to put an end to what they had condoned under the pretence of their blindness. They rose and overthrew the power that their corrupted leaders had managed to build behind their backs taking advantage of their lack of commitment.

The deposed tyrants' lives were spared, instead, they were sentenced to beggary and vagrancy to emphasise their incapacity. Moreover, as a way to keep alive the collective memory to avoid the repetition of such infamies, they were condemned with the worst punishment that can be given to those who want to die; they were sentenced to stay alive.

When the new day arrived, the inhabitants of "The Site" promised each other, among many other things, that being strong as they were they would never again be dominated by the weaker; that they would never again accept any kind of government whose first priorities were not the happiness and welfare of the human being as a whole; that they would never accept theories based on an alleged racial superiority; that never more would they discriminate others for their race, creed, sex or sexual orientation, or for any other reason. Furthermore, they also agreed that, since God had thousands of names, depending on the different cultures known by them, they would never again admit the superiority of one god over another, regardless his name, nor any interpretation of his teachings would be considered superior to any other. They also concurred that they would never allow any earthly power to claim its being the ministry of God because it was in the conscience and the heart of men where he dwelt. Finally, and most important of all, was their promise to never again pretend they were blind.

They regained control over their lives, with the decision to build them up again without hate and without fear, with sorrow for what they had lost but with faith in their future as well. Even though they knew the latter was uncertain, they were fully aware that it would depend only on their actions. They were no longer prepared to let others reinvent a future for them.

As a result of all these agreements and decisions, they started working together, shoulder to shoulder, whites, blacks, yellows, without any of them minding the colour of their skins, nor their religions. They all felt bound together by their common sense of loss. Their grief had brought with it a true sense of belonging to the place.

Now that they had understood that their place in the world was not the place where they had been born, but that in which they had chosen to die peacefully, and because they felt they were part of the place they inhabited, they decided to change its name. It would no longer be known as "The Site", from then onwards they would call it "Our Site".

This time, when they had taken responsibility for what had happened and, as they felt connected with each other because physical differences were no longer relevant, they also decided that they would no longer call themselves "Those from There", now they would be "Those from Here". This was their place and it was their duty to make it better.

They had realised that the only way to rebuild their lives and families was to accept with total humility the reality they had been bound to live and to respect that of the others, their equals.

They had also understood that no change is possible within any human group, if each of its members does not experience a personal change. Otherwise, it is like trying to control the forces of Nature, because, eventually, it will destroy all attempts made to this purpose. These forces can be channelled, as long as we learn to respect them and live in harmony with its laws, without trying to control them if these forces resist being controlled.

Besides themselves, they no longer had to fear anything nor anybody. They had known what there was on both sides of the mountains. They had also seen the dark side of the moon and had discovered that if the sun inhabits our hearts, it is more important than seeing it rise or set, to know how to look at it, and feel its presence alive in us.

Daybreak

I can be driven away from my path;
they can try to subdue my will.
But they can not stop me,
from the depth of my soul,
to choose what I want.
HENRIK JOHAN IBSEN

How much pain, and how much death I could see around me! How great has been my responsibility! I think no one, not even you or her, ever knew or will know. Such kind of secrets are destined to live within ourselves, and now and again will awake us to the terrible moments traversed, silently granting us, many times, the opportunity to repent and improve ourselves.

It was during those days that I understood that only because of having granted someone power over our lives, we start to fear him. It was because for the simple reason that I felt there was nothing else to lose, that I openly stopped fearing "We".

How many moments of anguish I had while I wondered how my family was doing; how could I manage to rest, between battles, without minding the remains of those who had been my equals! I had involuntarily lost comprehension of the tragedy in which I was submerged, as a form of escaping tragedy and to justify my actions.

Only the memory of happy moments in my life allowed me to recognise myself as a human, and in the same way, only the memory of my family allowed me to feel that my efforts to see them safe and sound would not make my death, if it so happened, be in vain.

How often did I conjure myself, among dreams, arriving home and seeing her waiting for me while my children, who were playing outside, ran into my arms as they soon as they recognised me!

How could I know what had happened to them? How could I not imagine it, when I had seen it in other townships, with other people, my fellows and equals? How could I surmise that we can be safe from the consequences of war, when it nestles in our hearts and we take part in it?

Our thirst for vengeance, generated by the same drive in others, only achieved the destruction of all that we desired to preserve. We wished ourselves blind not to see what was happening and not feel the danger, and as blind men we utterly destroyed all that was within our reach.

When they died, everything lost meaning to me... suffering... living.... the poem I wrote in the battlefield thinking of her, of our family, of the consequences this stupid war would have in our lives... in me.

My soul, beyond words,
Cries for you in the distance.
After the war
In our lives
Nothing will be the same,
Not the sky, or the stars,
Not dreams, or looks
Or silence, or words,
Or nights, or mornings,
Or waiting, or absence,

Or presence, or hope,

Or kisses, or caresses,

Nor the man who waits,

Or the woman who lingers on,

Nor the scents of the skin,

Or the brushing of hands,

Or the book, or the poem.

Everything has somehow changed

... Not even I am the man I used to be!

Nothing is the same.

But if one day when arriving,

Should you find me in armour

Do not hesitate, strip me of it!

Or if my doors are closed

Knock till they open!

Or if you see me building walls,

Talk to me, pull them down!

Or if you see me looking away,

Do not heed the course of my gaze!

Your presence will suffice, so that one by one,

My defences will crumble before you.

They were not built for you!

They were only erected to shield my soul,

And heal its wounds,

At the cost of isolation.

Like a warrior, guarding his weapons,

At times I alone... and my sword remain,

Awaiting that new dawn

When in our lives

There will be no more fighting.

My soul, beyond words,

Cries for you in the distance,

Though it sometimes feels

That waiting is important no more.

My love is comforted

By your memory and my hope

Because this shall not be, regardless war

Or distance,

My last poem for you

Nor shall I stop thinking of you, every morning.

We all had, unawares, lost the meaning of the word dignity.

However, during those hard days I understood that not everything was lost, that it was possible to hope for the day after, providing we made up our minds to look life in the face, by assuming the responsibility for our destiny.

It was in the North side of the city, on that particular day, in the midst of a fierce fight to defend, to attack, to survive; I was in the middle of probably one of the last combats when at a certain moment, wounded and trying to take shelter, I inexplicably found myself cut off and alone in the ruins of what not so long ago had been a home... maybe quite the same to what once had been their homes... or my home.

In that instant of fear, pain and utter exhaustion I could see, without being able to do anything to avoid it, how one of the warriors of "The Yellows" discovered my presence and started to run swiftly to where I was, with the clear intention of killing me, but, for no apparent reason, stopped short in front of me, lowering his weapon.

Fear and resignation for what I saw as my certain death, prevented me from understanding what was actually happening, until I could recognize the face of my friend Xi behind a grown beard and the thick grime and blood that covered his clothes and body.

Quickly glancing all around to make sure no one was looking or could hear us, he asked, almost inaudibly: "Pero, is that you?" , "Xi?" I retorted, by way of dispelling his doubts and mine.

Sitting together, looking into each other's eyes and touching each other fraternally, somehow wanting to express more than what words could say, he asked if I was badly hurt, at the same time he looked over my wounds with the resignation of one who knows he cannot be of any help at all.

After making sure that my state was not serious, we both asked, practically in unison "How're you?" "How's your family?" "D'you know anything about mine?" Then, we remained side by side, not making any more questions; our bodies resting on each other, as if yearning for those less violent times, when being together only meant joy for those moments that our friendship brought us.

I can't reckon how long we sat there, but at that moment, which seemed eternal, I understood that real friendship is often above misfortune. Xi and I had never been enemies; we were simply two friends, with identical ideals and interests, who had, just by chance, found themselves on enemy sides of a war.

Before parting, while Xi was busily hiding me among different objects, we promised each other that if any of us found any of our families, we would not only tell them we had seen each other safe, but also that, we would do anything within our power to protect and help them at any time.

All this happened before the fire started in the woodlands... the destruction of all that fire and man could produce... before peace was declared.

All this happened before I, on the way home, seeing the smoke that surged from what had been my neighbourhood, was gripped by anguish in my heart in anticipation of what I was about to see.

I will not tell you what I saw, or the profound pain I felt at that moment, because this feeling only belongs to me, and also because you would never understand it; because you have not felt it; nor have had that sensation of hollowness in your soul, while looking at those beings, which blindness had prevented you from protecting during all that time, butchered savagely ... maybe by those same men and weapons which were meant to defend them.

It was then, when feeling the loneliest and most vulnerable being on earth, that I discovered to what extremes ambition could sway men. My fury was indescribable when I witnessed how my leaders and those of "The Yellows" were making agreements concerning our own lives and possessions, which only favoured them, disregarding what had happened and the blood shed by many innocents in an effort to defend an idea which they had been taught to believe to be true.

My first reaction was to start running in fear, not knowing what else to do, but later, upon realizing that nothing could save me from certain death when falling into those hands, I made the decision to show in death the courage and dignity I had not been able to show in life.

What happened afterwards you already know because you witnessed it; in the same way as you have known that a voice in the midst of many other silent voices binds us to truth; just like a tiny match compels us to follow its light in a dark night; like dawn draws us to await the sun.

Epilogue

Consider your origins: you were not made that you might live as brutes, but so as to follow virtue and knowledge"
DANTE ALIGHIERI

Many times I have wondered if what I lived in "The Site" was real or just the product of my imagination or a dream. I think I will never find an answer to this, especially when taking into account that all human reality is always apparent.

I only know that because I once opposed the killing of other human beings, or because I denounced other deaths that could have been avoided, regardless cause or reason or corruptible absolute powers, and also because I spoke against the discrimination and the persecution suffered by countless people because of their creed, race, ideas, sexual choice, etc., today I find myself here. I have been labelled as dangerous, and placed under the custody of a system that in the name of the community won't spare expenses in their attempt to socialize me, and to this purpose use the resources they are denying to unprotected sectors.

Should I consider that being socialised means to put up with injustice without doing anything about it? Should I consider that being socialised is to pretend to be blind, like "Those from There" did to avoid sympathising with their neighbour's pain? Should I consider that being socialised is to remain indifferent to the hunger of many that could easily be avoided? How many other things beyond reason, should I condone and silence, to be regarded as a socialised person?

Is it that we have not understood yet that it is the silence of many and not the deeds of a few what has caused the great evils that affect us as a society, and that these have not been prevented because we have never seriously proposed ourselves to take action?

Is it that we have not understood that we are all part of what is known as a rational system, which is often ruled by irrational beings supported and held in power by our lack of commitment? Have we not yet realised that what in our system is regarded as normal is nothing but insanity taken by all as standard behaviour?

I resent thinking, like Pero thought, that our fate is to die for causes we know are unjust!

If I must agree to all this to obtain my freedom within this system, I prefer to die in it. They will never be able to confine or restrain my fighting spirit. They will never be able to deprive me of my real freedom, my internal freedom of thought, which is their most dangerous enemy! Truth, like smoke, eventually comes up, provided we can change our belief into concrete action!

As I have said before, many times I ask myself if what I lived in "The Site" is just a tale born from my imagination or from a dream. But I also wonder whether what was real was my life there and that this present is nothing but just one of my dreams. How can I tell one reality from the other when both have so much in common?

And if this was the dream, and one day, when I awoke in "The Site" I told everything I have seen here as "normal, actual and true", would I not be regarded as dangerous too?

I shall never be able to forget the causes and consequences that drove "The Site" to the situations it lived. How important is it whether everything was real or merely the product of my imagination, when all that happened there could likely happen here?

I shall never be able to erase from my memory the image of Pero, up there, on the tower, holding his dead son in his arms, challenging all the people with his words, and then plummeting towards the ground, mocking his fate, and justifying himself to empty souls.

Because I was deeply moved by its words, I will never forget the poem he recited shortly before his death. I managed to get hold of it among his clothes and read it between pushes and shoves before they grabbed it and took it away, together with Pero's body.

It was called *The Victory* and it is quite possible that it was passed on to him by his parents, for it was written in the 19th Century by a poet called Ricardo Gutierrez, from a place on the other side of the mountains known as Argentina.

In view of the fact that I believe we have learned so little in such a long time, I shall never get tired of saying it, waiting for the moment to go to sleep again, and recite it all over again in my dreams.

> Alas! Don't sing a song of victory
> On the sunless day of battle
> When you've slashed your brother's forehead
> With the damned blow of your blade.
> When the pigeon in the sky is felled,
> The perched dove shivers on the branch;
> When the fierce tiger is abated on the plain
> The frightful beasts hush in their fright.
> And you sing hymns of victory
> On the sunless day of fight?
> O, man alone on this heathen world
> Can sing when men around him fall;
> I cannot cheer when my brother dies.
> Brand me infamous with the burning iron,
> Because on the day your gore is spurting
> From my shaky hand the harp falls down.

Today, you and I have told our stories that, like many others, may seem to many either real or fictitious ... And what if it was not so? What if what we have told did really happen, on a different level of time or space?

It may be that we are neither past, nor future, nor present. Maybe we are only a thought that merely wanders along time, retelling what we have had to live, as a way to define the moment where we currently are.

Honestly, I believe that we must not, that you must not, ask so many questions. Maybe it is like they say Buddha expressed: "All that we are is the result of what we have thought. All that we are arises with our thoughts". Can it be we are just the materialization of our ideas?

Once things are over, when we narrate different events we realise that their happening may have taken years, according to the conventional method devised by men to measure time and be able to determine the chronology and dates of the different occurrences in their lives. However, they have crossed our minds at a pace that doesn't differ from this convened time.

What if we were minute particles of another world or of something much bigger, beyond our understanding? If, for example, we were nano-creations and our nano-world was ruled by different parameters and/or scales beyond our knowledge and comprehension?

And if our stories, those we have told in this book, were not only real, but also complementary? And if what both of us believe were dreams, actually had happened in parallel worlds and both were real?

Is not "our reality", everything we regard and deem as certain which, after all, actually is apparent?

What if your story was actually my dream, and my story the real one and you just a product of my thoughts? And if neither had I died nor had you dreamt? And, if both of us were the creation of someone else and, therefore, a way to describe his world? Wouldn't we in that case be real too? Wouldn't we be a means to give entity to his ideas? If such were the case, which of the worlds described by the author would be the real one for him – his, yours, mine, or the three of them at the same time?

Have you ever thought that it may be that we are not the substance that creates the ethereal, but rather a part of the ethereal that can create the substance? What if we were just living thought?

Maybe this story is nothing but fiction, both for you and for me, and for the one who is writing it, or for the one who is reading it.

And if this reader were also the corporeal representation of somebody else's thought, alien to us? And if there was a fifth, a sixth or a seventh one, and so on?

Could this be the reason why certain people are more concerned in controlling our minds rather than our bodies, because the latter are of no practical use for them?

We may also wonder if thought were the real thing and the body pure imagination. Is it not possible to think that definitely we are nothing but one energy controlled by another, and that in this game of control and no control both their fates are to generate new energies capable of creating or destroying everything on their way?

It is for all this that we must learn that our road to happiness always goes through our thoughts and not through events outside them. Everything is a concept that, in one way or another, will be expressed by our actions.

Just like we cannot master the winds, no one will be able to silence our voices, though be they silent, because if there were one single person to oppose inequality and injustice, that voice would resound on our consciences much more loudly than thousands of voices incapable of uttering a sound.

"The Site" can be your site and "We" can also be a product of your own creation. It is left to you to let things happen the way you shape them in your thoughts. Only through commitment, courage and hope we may, some day, achieve a better world.